RETURN TO TEBEL-AYR
THE JOURNEY CONTINUES

RETURN TO TEBEL-AYR

THE JOURNEY CONTINUES

Colleen K. Snyder

BROADMAN PRESS
NASHVILLE, TENNESSEE

© Copyright 1993 ● Broadman Press
All rights reserved
4260-58
ISBN: 0-8054-6058-6
Dewey Decimal Classification: F
Library of Congress Card Catalog Number: 92-19565
Printed in the United States of America
Library of Congress Cataloging-in-Publication Data
Snyder, Colleen K., 1954-
 Return to Tebel-Ayr : the journey continues / Colleen
K. Snyder
 p. cm.
 ISBN: 0-8054-6058-6
 PS3569.N85R48 1993
 813'.54--dc20

92-19565
CIP

To the memory of
Brooks Robert Snyder
father-in-law, friend, and
brother in the Lord

We love you, Dad

Special thanks to Sandy Ford
for her extraordinary ability at
deciphering hieroglyphics
and for helping with the typing

Contents

New Directions

Nathan Adamson blinked back the tears that threatened to blur his last look at his sleeping children. Rachel and Jonathan slept soundly on the cave floor, too exhausted by their perilous escape from Tebel-Ayr to care about the hardness of their "beds." A small fire burned brightly near the cave entrance, making the cavern glow softly. Packs and supplies for the journey ahead were neatly stowed against one wall. But it was a journey Nathan would not be taking with them. Not this time.

Nathan stroked Rachel's cheek lovingly, gently. At twenty, she was no longer his little girl but a woman. Nathan touched her brown hair lightly. Her hair had always matched his own color until recently. Now his was streaked in gray and white, as his fifty years caught up with him. Nathan bit his lip, then whispered, "I love you, Rachel." He kissed her carefully, then turned away quickly, half stumbling in his pain. Faith. Trust. Faith . . . .

Nathan gathered himself and moved across the cave to where Jonathan was snoring. Doubt for his son ate at him. Would the nineteen-year-old make it across Yada into the safety of Amanah? Jon, who not-so-secretly hated the very mention of the King whom Nathan served. Was it possible he would ever come to serve Haben Jah? How? How?

Faith. Trust. Faith . . . . Nathan reached his son's side and stopped. There was so much Nathan wanted to say, and now there was no time to say it. Nathan knelt down beside Jon and ran his hand across the young man's head one last time. Doubt and fear began to rise, but Nathan quelled them. Neshamah would not order the children brought to Yada now if the time were not right. And Ha-ben Jah would not leave them until all that could be done had been done to save them. Even in spite of themselves, if need be. Faith. Nathan hesitated, then bent forward and kissed Jon's forehead. "I love you, Jon." Jon roused slightly, turned over, and continued snoring.

Resolved, Nathan stood up and faced the silent guide who waited patiently in the darkened cave entrance. "Take good care of them, Nahal."

The guide nodded and stepped forward. Nathan set his shoulders, drew a deep breath, and walked outside into the darkness. He did not look back.

The storm had subsided; a gentle breeze replaced the shrieking winds that had fought the family earlier that evening. Nathan walked purposefully back to the river Irijah. The wide torrent they had crossed with such ca-lamity was gone. A quiet, narrow stream lay before him. Nathan said softly, "Getting across is always hardest. Once over, it's never the same again."

"For those who trust the King."

Nathan smiled, and he turned to face the man who strode to meet him. "Neshamah. Thank You for coming."

Neshamah looked to be about sixty, but Nathan knew better. The man was ageless. His face, his bearing, his voice all hinted at great power, but power that was con-trolled and veiled. Few ever saw Kadosh Neshamah fully revealed. The man said, "I am with you always, Ben-'el."

"I know, Neshamah. But it seems there are times You are more 'with me' than others."

Neshamah smiled. "When you attend to Me more, you are more aware of me."

"Then You have my full attention." Nathan motioned to a far-off glow across the river. "You said You had words for me before I returned to Tebel-Ayr."

"Yes."

"New counsel?"

"No, Ben-'el. Reminders of truth you already know." The two men began walking toward the stream. As they reached its banks, the Irijah parted silently. Neshamah and Nathan crossed on dry ground, stepped up the other side and kept going. Behind them the Irijah resumed its flow, burbling joyfully on its way.

Neshamah spoke calmly. "Trials there will be. In this world you will have tribulation. But be of good cheer; I have overcome the world."

Nathan said softly, "So it was said."

"And so it is. Adam Chata does not rule of his own accord. His persecution of you and the Chasidim is but for a time, and for a season. He will not prevail."

"In the end, I know. But for now . . . ." Nathan looked at his guide. "For now, how should we live?"

"As before Haben Jah Himself."

Nathan considered all that this was simple statement would mean. "As You say, Neshamah. My times are in Your hands."

Neshamah smiled. "From eternity your times have been in My hands, Ben-'el. You merely did not not realize it until recently."

Nathan laughed. "Very recently, I'm afraid." Neshamah did not answer, except with the twinkle in his coal black eyes. Nathan changed the subject. "When I get back to the city, where should I go?"

"That will be made clear in time."

"Your time?"

"Yes."

"Then I'll wait."

"You have learned well, Ben-'el."

"I hope so." Silently they marched closer to the glow of Tebel-Ayr, queen city of Golah, and the heart of darkness.

Within the palace of Biyrah, Governor Adam Chata

paced angrily back and forth across his chambers. The plush scarlet carpet muffled the sound of his marching but did nothing to cushion his anger. The short, stocky man waved his fists in frustration. He muttered through clenched teeth, "Will no one deliver me of these infidels? Why must every advance I make be challenged by these zealots? Can't they see what I offer them? How dare they refuse my grace!" The intricately woven tapestries hanging on the walls muffled his shouts. He whirled around and glared at the man standing in the doorway. Chata bellowed, "You! You swore you'd convert the Chasidim; swore you could convince them to leave off their opposition. Instead they grow more unyielding! What of your great education reforms, Ramah? Marvelous information campaigns! Wonderful training programs! Trash, Ramah. All of it useless trash."

Ben Ramah stepped cautiously into the room, assessing his Governor's mood. Ben was good at assessing moods. His ability to quickly and accurately read a situation, then turn it to his best advantage was legendary. It was a talent that had served him admirably during his time in Tebel-Ayr. Aided by his intelligence, his charm, and his striking good looks, Ben Ramah had swiftly risen to power. Five feet ten, thick, light-brown hair, hazel eyes that seemed to change color to meet his moods . . . Ramah was aptly fitted for the position of Governor's adjutant.

The last four years under Adam Chata had been the most challenging for him. Adam Chata's moods shifted hourly and reading the man wrong was an ever-present danger. But Ben Ramah did it better at thirty than men who had been with the Governor his entire life—all sixty years of it. Ben knew that the Governor had been out among the people again that day. He'd been scheduled to visit one of the new care centers in the heart of the city. Since Adam Chata went nowhere unannounced, it was an easy guess that some of the more vocal Chasidim had confronted him. Ramah shook his head slightly, visualizing the too-common scenario. The beneficent Chata, cuddling small children, chanting favorite rhymes with the classes, directing the flow of the children's spiritual energies . . . then having the session disrupted by one or more of the zealots. From the intensity of Adam Chata's agitation, it must have been one of the more extreme devoteés. Probably some misguided fool tried to cast a demon out of the Governor. It happened all the time.

Ben spoke guardedly. "Not all has been useless, Governor. The Chasidim still exist, but their numbers have been steadily declining. They make fewer and fewer converts because of our programs. Because we train the children so effectively in our truths, even their own children reject their teachings. As long as we are patient and exercise restraint, I predict that the entire sect will die out in two generations."

Chata stopped his pacing only inches from Ben's face, "You predict? Two generations? What good does that do me now? I don't want to wait two generations. I want them stopped now, do you hear? Now!!"

Ramah objected, "Governor, throughout their history, these people have been persecuted. Every time they suffer persecution, they resist more and more. The more they resist, the stronger their faith becomes. Their numbers increase when they are persecuted. During periods of relative peace and prosperity, we are able to make inroads against their religious fanaticism. When our programs removed the need of people to search for 'something better,' or 'something more,' as they say, we removed the need for Haben Jah. If we give them heaven on earth, then they won't need to look for heaven anywhere else. And it is working, sir. My informants have reported a dramatic drop in attendance at the Chasidim houses. If you will stay the course we have set, the whole problem will die out."

Ben saw his leader calm noticeably as he talked. He thought briefly that perhaps he was making progress.

But very briefly. Adam Chata seized on Ramah's unfortunate choice of pronouns and seethed, "*We* are making inroads against them? *We* removed the need for Haben Jah? *We* give them heaven? *We* set the course?" Ben's eyes widened as he realized his error. Chata continued, "*We* have done nothing, Ramah. *I* have given the Chasidim everything, everything their archaic beliefs demand. I did. Not we, not you, or anyone else. I did. Never, never forget that."

Ben nodded. "Yes, sir."

Chata mimicked sarcastically, "Yes, sir." He glared hard at Ben. "You say it with your lips, but your heart is far from me. You call me master, but you don't obey me."

Ben protested, "Governor, I have never . . . ."

"Spare me your innocence. You seem to forget that I read the hearts of men. Why do you think I was able to become Governor of Golah so quickly? Charm and good looks?" Chata laughed harshly. "I look on the inside of people. I know their wants, their desires, their perceptions. And I know how to meet them." Chata stalked to the windows that overlooked the city of Tebel-Ayr. He stared out at the teeming center of commerce below him.

The queen city came into her full glory at night. Corner lamplights gave a pink hue to the fog, which softened the edges of the thousand buildings. Only foot traffic was allowed in the streets; a few handcarts, an occasional peddler with a larger wagon, but nothing more. The business of Tebel-Ayr was people: their education, enlightenment, and enjoyment. Reading rooms were strategically located on every block, fully stocked with Adam Chata's recommended titles for the "well-rounded individual."

Coupled to the reading rooms were government-sponsored pleasure houses, where every man, woman, boy, or girl could do what felt right in his or her own eyes. "If it feels good, do it" was the operating phrase. The popularity of the houses provided Adam Chata with the bulk of his labor force. One day's work, one day's pleasure. An equitable exchange, and lines were long to serve the Governor. No matter the job, whether sweeping the grounds of the palace, washing windows, digging gardens, or building new centers, Adam Chata had a ready and willing work force.

Spiritual centers came next, for those less interested in the purely physical pursuits. Guidance, direction, information, all could be obtained through the wisdom of the ancient ones. Each center was directed by a government appointee, handpicked by Adam Chata himself. Government license ensured that no wayward influence affected the people of Golah. Only the Governor's truth was taught here.

The remainder of the city was devoted to schools—all government licensed and approved, with a curriculum carefully designed to meet the needs of the individual.

Adam Chata lectured to Ben, "Never, never give people what they want. It only makes them think they want more. Material possessions are not what satisfy. The trick is to alter people's perceptions. Help them see that they already have it all, right where they are. The nakedest child in the emptiest hovel has everything he will ever need or want. What we must do is show him his inner self. Show him his own potential, his own greatness, his own god-given god-likeness. Show him he is god, and he'll spend the rest of his life indebted to you for showing him the road to happiness and fulfillment. Teach him the greatest lesson of all: that he is totally responsible for himself, and never, never let him think otherwise. Reality is what you make it. Joy comes from you. You have the keys to your own fulfillment. That's what I gave them. And that's why I'm the head of Tebel-Ayr. I gave the common man what he wanted most. I gave him back his soul."

Adam Chata had calmed down, finally, soothed by his own exhortations. He turned and faced Ben Ramah. "The problem with the Chasidim is that they refuse to accept responsibility for themselves. They want someone else to carry their burdens. They are locked into their teachings about a savior and a sacrifice. You don't understand them, Ramah. Not like I do. They want a sacrifice." Chata's eyes glistened suddenly, and Ben could clearly see the ideas forming in his Governor's head. "A sacrifice and a savior. That's it. That's it exactly. And I know just how to make it work."

To Ben's consternation, the Governor began to laugh. Adam Chata threw back his head and crowed, "It's perfect! Brilliant! Inspired! I am so brilliant!"

Abruptly Adam Chata stopped cold and stared hard at Ben. "And you will be the one to make it work. My most trusted and loyal lieutenant, you will carry out my plan."

Ben nodded. "Of course, Governor. I have always executed your orders."

Adam Chata snickered. "Executed, hmmm? Prophetic choice of words, my son! Now listen. Here is what *we* are going to do."

Kadosh Neshamah

Dawn glimmered in the east as Nathan and Neshamah drew within sight of Tebel-Ayr. The trip back from the Irijah had covered some twenty miles, yet surprisingly Nathan was not tired. The country between the river and the city was relatively flat, with few bushes or rocks to bar the way. Walking through the wilds, spending quiet hours with the Guide Himself left the man feeling refreshed and calm. Even the challenge of the wall ahead did not seem insurmountable, regardless of the fear that nibbled at him.

The wall was a relic from ages past, a time when security was measured solely by strength and numbers. It circled all of Tebel-Ayr, a distance of over three hundred miles. Twenty feet high, eight feet wide, it was constructed of a material that was a favorite of the ancients, but whose composition had been lost and forgotten over time. Without seam or joint, its cold gray surface absorbed rather than reflected light. It was a true marvel, a monument to a people whose technical expertise had outdistanced their maturity. There were other remnants of the old world, but the wall was far and away the most impressive.

Neshamah led Nathan to the southernmost portal, then stopped. Five Tabbach guards lounged near the entrance. Gate patrol duty was a lowly assignment, usually given as punishment for sub-par performance. This unit was no different. Their uniforms reflected their attitudes: open black tunics, gray shirts half-tucked-in, unwashed pants, and boots that hadn't been polished for months. Their staffs, symbols of authority, were scattered on the ground. The guards were obviously bored; two were asleep, two were playing cards spread between them. Only the fifth man was watching the countryside, searching for something he alone could see. Guarding the gates was as futile a job as there was in the queen city. Without the proper papers people left the protection of Tebel-Ayr at their own peril. No sensible person ever wanted to leave, anyway. Everyone knew that Tebel-Ayr was the center of freedom for all, the model of peace, prosperity, joy, and self-fulfillment. Why should anyone want to abandon that? Thousands lived contentedly within her borders. Only the deluded or deranged would try to leave. And if someone were deluded enough to try to leave, he was obviously a danger to himself or others and needed to be confined.

Neshamah stopped just out of earshot of the guards and instructed Nathan, "When you have reentered Tebel-Ayr, go to the house of Leah Bataqab. I have instructed her to expect a visitor."

Nathan asked, "Is she one of the Chasidim? I don't remember hearing her name before."

"You have not, yet she will provide for you. Do not return to your old dwelling; the soldiers have seized all you possessed. They are watching for your return."

"What do I do?"

Neshamah said quietly. "Live and wait. Your responsibilities will be clear to you."

"Where does this woman live?"

"Not far from Bavith. On the street Taqan, the third house from the corner. Look for the kiymah in the window."

"A kiymah? She's of the 'Ibriy?"

"Leah is My child, Ben-'el."

Nathan acknowledged the rebuke immediately. "As You say, Neshamah."

"I do. Come, we must be going."

Nathan saw a new squad of five soldiers approach the gate: the morning guard. There would be general confusion and even greater inattentiveness during the change of shifts. Neshamah nodded, then stepped forward. Nathan followed close behind his Guide.

No guard looked up, at, or near the two men. Neshamah and Nathan passed through the squads as easily as they had passed through the Irijah. Nathan couldn't help holding his breath, though he knew he was safe. He did, however, resist the temptation to reach out and touch one of the guards. The command from the Kathab had been reinforced by Haben Jah Himself when He was tempted by Heylel: "You will not test the Lord your God." Nathan walked quickly, but in awe. It was one thing to know intellectually that Neshamah was capable of such feats. It was another to believe in your heart that He would do such things when the need arose. But to actually see it, to be the recipient of a miracle . . . that was something else entirely.

Nathan followed Neshamah past the guard post, down a deserted lane, then into the emptiness between the wall and the city proper. The first rays of the morning light filtered through the perpetual haze that shrouded Tebel-Ayr. It made for beautiful sunrises and sunsets, but left the remainder of the day in a gray fog. Not that many of the inhabitants noticed or cared. When the focus of life was predominantly the self, one rarely had time to be concerned with sunsets. The citizens of Tebel-Ayr were continually exhorted to look inward; to focus on developing their minds, souls, and spirits. Anything outside the self was a distraction. Besides, the fog was was what you made it, anyhow. See it in a different perspective, and it could be a friend.

Nathan shook his head. He muttered, "Half a mile inside the wall, and already the old way of thinking is back. Lord King, protect me."

Nathan stopped suddenly, closed his eyes and bowed his head. He whispered, "Lord King, ignore me, but please, please protect Rachel and Jon. Be with them and guide them to Your Truth. Nothing I do means anything if they don't reach You. Help them."

Nathan stood silently a moment, then straightened up and looked around. Neshamah was gone. Nathan half-nodded. Gone, but not really. Nathan set his shoulders and marched toward the buildings ahead. "Go to the street which is called Taqan and inquire for one Leah Bataqab." Nathan frowned. He was puzzled at his instructions. The 'Ibriy and the Chasidim were not always, well . . . how should he put it? Not kindly affectioned to one another? Though both traced their roots to the same King, Lord of all creation and often served Him with equal zeal, the matter of Haben Jah stood between them. Of course, it was the matter of Haben Jah that stood between the Chasidim and the rest of the world. But while the rest of the world might freely acknowledge Haben's existence without feeling any particular obligation or animosity, the 'Ibriy could not. The claims of Haben Jah struck at the very soul of their being. Nathan walked on.

Ben Ramah sat in his silent office, staring morosely at his desk. The intricate stone inlay patterns normally aided his creative processes. But now, they just lay there. They'd been laying there all night, staring back at him, waiting for him to come up with something. Ben shook his head. Come up with what? Chata was insane. That was all it could be—insanity. The Governor had given bizarre orders before, and somehow Ben had made them work. When Chata decided that every third hour of the business day should be devoted to meditation and prayer, Ben had managed to sell it to the owners as good for business and as a means of increasing productivity and profit. When the Governor wanted to have national holidays in honor of his ancestors, Ben had found a way and even made sure

the general populace took it seriously. But this time . . .
Ramah shook his head. There was no mistaking the command, though. Adam Chata wanted Kadosh Neshamah
captured and brought under control.

Captured? Controlled? Insane. How do you capture
someone whom no one but Chasidim were convinced even
existed? To be sure, there were others who spoke of having seen Him, or having experienced His presence, or felt
His impact on their lives. But only the Chasidim claimed
to know Him face-to-face. Ramah had always dismissed
them as the lunatic fringe. Most Habenists had abandoned belief in Neshamah, and even in Haben Himself,
years ago.

Ben would have liked to take credit for this advance in
self-actualization, but he couldn't. Belief in Haben had
waned long before Ramah had been born. He'd only
helped orchestrate the systematic elimination of its final
strains from the society around him. Adam Chata may
have denigrated Ramah's educational reforms, but anyone of vision knew the true future of an idea lay in the
coming generations. Teach them properly while they are
young, and they are yours for life. Ben had heard a Haben
cultist say once, "Train a child in the way he should go,
and when he is old, he will not depart from it." Remark-
able logic from an anachronistic zealot.

Ben sighed. All well and good, of course, but hardly use-
ful now. Capture Neshamah. How? The man—if man he
was—had no center of operations, gave no schedule of ap-
pearances, had no regular routines of any kind. He came
and went like the wind. How do you capture the wind?
Ben felt frustration blocking his thought processes. If
Adam Chata had ordered it, then Ben could do it. There
had to be a way. But how? No answers came. He could . . .
no, he couldn't. Maybe if he . . . no, that wouldn't work,
either. There was always a chance . . . no. Ben pondered
and pondered, but nothing came to mind. Finally, after
another hour of useless brainstorming he sat back in his

chair and closed his eyes. Ben visualized himself walking down a darkened tunnel. It was the passage from his present confusion and mental paralysis to the regions of the mind where answers freely flowed, and realities were altered to reflect innovative solutions to any and all difficulties. Ben felt himself relaxing as he exercised the familiar rituals. His mind began working again. State the objective. (Never call it a problem. A problem is a negative view of a positive reality. There are no problems, only opportunities for growth.)

Objective: to capture, control, and/or eliminate Kadosh Neshamah. A properly stated objective had to be obtainable. To capture Neshamah was to first admit he existed. Very well, then, back up a step. First he had to convince himself Neshamah was real. What evidence was there that Neshamah lived? Who was He, anyhow? Ben slowed in his tunnel, still in the darkness. He couldn't honestly say he knew who Neshamah was, or claimed to be. Or was claimed to be by the Chasidim. Ben would have to find out more about Him. Learn the truth about Kadosh Neshahmah.

For one instant the tunnel blazed brightly. Then the darkness swallowed the light, and the walls of Ben's mental passage began to crash and boom around him, reverberating with the echoes of Adam Chata's thundering, "Truth? Truth is what I make it, what I say it is! You fool!! There is no truth outside of your present reality. And I am the only reality that matters!!"

In his mind a towering image of Adam Chata glowered before Ramah. Waves of malevolent power, of anger and hatred flowed from the menacing presence, enveloping the hapless man. Ben fell to his knees under the onslaught, unable to lift even his eyes. The flaming spirit roared, "You exist to serve only me! I am your guide, your master, your conscious existence. I am your way, your truth, and the only life you will ever know. Never imagine there is anyone or anything else. Do you hear me?

Never! Never!" Chata disappeared, leaving only the echoes of his bellowing behind.

Shaken, Ben opened his eyes slowly, half-expecting to see Adam Chata standing in his office. But he was alone; the office was empty. His hands were shaking and he was breathing fast. He felt faint. He tried to collect his thoughts. It took nearly ten minutes before he was under control and again facing the "opportunity" before him. Capture Neshamah. How? Ben chose to blank out all he'd received from his previous creative meditation. There had been that one glimmer of light, though. Maybe he should save the idea and learn all he could about Neshamah. Ben rationalized quickly, almost defensively, "Even assassins get to know their victims."

Where should he start his research? Books? Ben chuckled. "We banned them all, you fool. Or rewrote them." What about asking someone who knew Neshamah? "Pardon me, sir, do you know Kadosh Neshamah?" Wise men would deny it; the Chasidim would boast of it but would refuse to talk to him. Not much help there, either.

From nowhere a thought occurred to him: *Read the Kathab.* Ben stopped cold at the idea. But before his conditioned fear responses could veto the thought, logic began to pour in. Why not? The Kathab was the most treasured book of the Chasidim. It spoke clearly of Kadosh Neshamah, told who He was, where He came from, what He came to do, what He was doing now. It was all there, nice and neat and in print for him. If Ben had the courage to read it. Really read it. If Ramah wanted to know the truth, it was all there.

Ben cringed slightly at the reminder of the concept of truth. But his thoughts continued. What was wrong with the idea? Ben wasn't afraid of a book, was he? He'd sworn all along there was nothing of consequence in it, no truth to any of its claims. Of course, he'd never read it. If he wanted to understand the Chasidim and help eliminate them and Neshamah, maybe he should get to know his enemy. The Kathab was the place to start.

The idea frightened Ramah, yet his fear puzzled him. Ben got up and went to the portrait of Adam Chata that hung on the far wall. Ignoring his Governor's beneficent countenance, Ben moved the picture aside and unlocked a small door hidden behind it. Inside the compartment were papers Ben had rescued from Adam Chata's files, saved for possible future reference. They contained incriminating records that Ben could use against anyone who tried to challenge him. There were also a few personal momentos, neatly preserved reminders of earlier innocence. A three-inch stuffed brown bear. A broken leather leash. Several crude charcoal sketches of a young woman.

Ben picked up the bear carefully and smiled. Tender memories stirred, reminders of who Ben had once been. A loyal friend, long ago. Chalaq and Ben, Ben and Chalaq. Teachers said they were inseparable. You saw one, you saw both. Chalaq had given him the bear when Ben was ten. "A watch-bear," he'd said. "He'll watch between us." And he had, too. For the next ten years he'd watched. He'd have gone on watching, but for the choices grownups make. Ben threw in with Adam Chata, Chalaq joined the Chasidim. So much for friendships.

Ben put the bear down carefully. He could never bring himself to discard the old fellow, though the friendship was long gone. Maybe it was because Ben wanted to believe he could be a loyal friend again. Some day. Some day when he was through climbing over people to reach the top. When life would again be for enjoyment, not conquest. When pleasures were . . . .

Ben shut the thoughts down. Maybe someday. Not today. Today there were challenges. Move on, move ahead. Move . . . .

Ben fingered the leather of the leash. Broken leash, broken promise. He'd kept it as a spur to remind himself that you get in this life only what you give yourself. Depend on others, and they will disappoint you every time. All he wanted was a pet, a dog. His father had promised him one, once he got settled. 'Ab Ramah was a teacher, prophet, and guide. It was his commission to travel from town to town bringing enlightenment to the masses. He was seldom home. On those rare occasions when he did return, 'Ab would remain locked in his room, studying, meditating, receiving the new light he was to share. Woe unto the man—or child—who disturbed 'Ab Ramah's studies! A dog would be an unnecessary distraction. But Ben wanted a pet. And what Ben wanted, Ben got. Sort of. Ben fingered the leash again. It wasn't easy to teach a lizard to heel. "Fetch" was even harder. The three-foot monster was good at "play dead," though.

Ben placed the leash next to the bear. He carefully avoided the drawings. Some memories were too painful. He was far enough removed from the bear and the lizard to be able to smile, now, and selectively remember the good times. But not for the girl. Not yet. She had filled his life. Could have gone on filling it, but for ambition. Whose ambition was unimportant. Move on, move ahead. Move

. . . .

Ben picked up the one item of contraband that could jeopardize his future with Chata's government. Yet ironically it was the one item that could right now help him preserve that future.

Ben dug out a leather-bound book; its condition pristine in spite of its age. It had been given to him when he was still a child, though he'd never read it. Or opened it. Or touched it. An eccentric aunt gave it to him; one of the Chasidim in spite of all family connections to the contrary. Aunt Dodavah had always been the black sheep of the family, one of those skeletons hidden neatly from public scrutiny. Ben didn't know what finally became of the old woman. He'd saved the book for one reason alone: it was his. The commotion over its bequest had made Ben aware of its special qualities, even at the age of six. His parents' almost violent opposition to the gift had made him that much more determined to keep it. Ben had ever been a child of strong will, so keep it he had. For twenty-four years he'd kept it hidden from parents, from classmates and teachers, from inquisitors, and from government officials. Even when he'd been responsible for collecting and destroying such hazardous material, he'd preserved his own copy. Now it was time to find out what all the fuss was about.

Ben carefully tucked the book into his satchel, then locked and covered the safe. He restored Adam Chata's portrait to its smiling prominence, then went back to his desk. He picked up several reports he was working on, along with correspondence from various organizations requesting various responses on various issues . . . none of which mattered in the least, now. Ben stuffed the sheaf of papers into his bag, grabbed his coat , and walked out of the office.

The ceremonial guard at the door stiffened to attention at Ben's appearance. Ben's young aide was seated at his desk, directly in front of Ben's door. Athariym's primary job was to see that Ben wasn't disturbed. Ben's unwillingness to give up control of all but the most menial duties kept the young man bored—and frustrated. Athariym looked up with surprise. "I didn't realize you were here, yet. What time did you come in?"

Ben ignored the question and said flatly, "I'm leaving for . . . awhile. Maybe a few days or so. I have a special assignment from the Governor. Don't look for me unless . . . ." Ben stopped, then said, "Don't look for me."

Athariym nodded, accustomed to his boss's erratic departures. "Yes, sir."

"Good." Ben Ramah left.

The House of Leah Bataqab

Nathan reached Bavith by mid-afternoon and had little difficulty locating the appointed house. In a neighborhood of look-alike conservatism, Leah Bataqab's stood out. It was brightly painted, eschewing the moderate grays and buffs of the day. (Colors were, after all, matters of personal preference. It was uncharitable to disturb your neighbor's sensitivities with your own selfish outward displays. Decorate the interior all you wish, but don't disturb the peace.)

The kiymah blazed proudly in both windows and above the front entrance. The bright symbol of the rayed sun identified Leah Bataqab as one of the 'Ibriy. Once a required form of identification used for discrimination and death, the Kiymah was now revered, even envied, as a mark of privilege. Though some might scoff at ancient superstitions, wiser heads grudgingly acknowledged that no people long survived who opposed the 'Ibriy. Whether it was because of their unique relationship to the King, as the 'Ibriy maintained, or for some other purpose known only to the ancients, the 'Ibriy as a people outlasted all who sought to destroy them. Wise was the government—or governor—who sought the favor of the 'Ibriy.

The triple star, though, marked Leah Bataqab as an individualist. One Kiymah was sufficient. Two was suspicious. Three was definitely trouble.

Nathan frowned. So, Leah Bataqab was both an 'Ibriy and an individualist, unafraid of or unsympathetic to the party line. That meant she was watched by the Tabbach, which could mean this place was a danger to him. Nathan hesitated, then drew himself up. Neshamah had sent him here. Haben Jah hadn't promised His followers ease and comfort, security and safety in their surroundings. He had only promised an opportunity for service and a pledge to be with them whatever came. Nathan recalled a passage from the Kathab, "through the fire, through the water." He nodded to himself. Through, not away from. Very well, through it was. Nathan stepped forward, raised his hand to knock, then stopped again. What was he to say? "Hi, Neshamah sent me?" True, but not necessarily advisable. Nathan prayed silently, "Lord King, direct me. What should I say?"

A second time the answer returned, "Neshamah sent me."

Nathan looked around surreptitiously, shrugged, and asked inwardly, "What?"

"Neshamah sent me."

Nathan grimaced. Direct and to the point. So be it. He knocked twice, then waited.

There was a moment's silence, then a woman's voice called, "It's open. Come in."

Nathan pushed the door open, stepped inside, then looked around in amazement. The layout of the house was traditional. The door opened on a small living room. A narrow hall branched off the left, leading to sleeping and eating quarters in the back. Compact, serviceable, simple basic housing. Traditional. But untraditional were the brightly colored canvases which hung everywhere, suspended even from the ceiling. There were paintings of glowing sunrises (or sunsets, it was hard to tell which.) There were vibrant landscapes filled with trees, shining waterfalls, and streams so lively Nathan could almost hear them gurgling. He saw portraits, children mostly, but some women and men. One powerful portrait stood out from the rest. It was a man, rugged, dark, black eyes dancing and smiling. He was clothed in simple garments, peasant style, and was built like a man accustomed to hard work. On his face was a look of pure joy. The man was laughing. His arms were outstretched, welcoming all comers. Nathan studied the picture intently, then whispered reverently, "Haben Jah, my Lord."

Movement caught his attention from the portrait. He turned as a young woman, perhaps twenty-two, no more than twenty-five, entered the room. She was short, barely five feet, with deep brown hair cut close to her face. She wore a painter's smock over a light gray shift. Again Nathan was struck by the contrasts: the basics, overlaid by the unconventional.

The woman wiped her hands on a paint-spattered rag, then held out one hand to Nathan and smiled broadly. "Welcome, Brother. Good to have you here." Her voice was strong and confident, as though she'd been expecting him.

Nathan shook her hand cautiously. "Thank you. Are you Leah Bataqab?"

The woman's smile faded slightly. She eyed Nathan a moment, then said, "You're not one of the regular committee members."

Nathan shook his head. "No, I'm not. Which committee?"

"Uncle Nadiyb's committee for the reformation and restoration of Leah Bataqab to the status quo."

"No."

"I thought not. They know who I am." She eyed Nathan again. "Then who are you?"

"Nathan Adamson. I was sent by . . . ." Nathan hesitated, then said evenly, "By Kadosh Neshamah."

Leah sighed. "Another one."

"Excuse me?"

"Never mind."

There was a moment's silence. Nathan asked, "Do you want to withdraw your welcome?"

Leah laughed. "No, of course not. Misguided though you may be, you are still welcome."

"Then I still thank you."

Leah motioned to her surroundings. "Make yourself at home, if you can."

Nathan smiled. "This is . . . unique. I've not seen talent like yours since . . . ." Nathan trailed off.

"Since the government banned public art?"

"Actually, since before that. Public art was never like this."

Leah cocked her head. "Like what?"

"Real."

"Ah, I see." Leah nodded knowingly. "You're one of the Chasidim."

"Why do you say that?"

"Only the Chasidim are concerned with 'real.' "

Nathan pointed to a picture of children dancing in a large circle. "And you aren't? Concerned with reality, I mean?"

Leah shook her head roughly. "Of course not. I am only interested in art." She fingered the painting Nathan had indicated, then asked softly, "Besides, where in Golah do you ever see children dancing?" She motioned to a waterfall. "Or see water running free?" She jerked her head towards a stunning seascape, with a flock of gulls whirling high above crashing waves. "Or see birds? Does any of that look real to you?"

Nathan said quietly, "Perhaps not in Golah. But I've seen them, Leah Bataqab. Obviously so have you, somewhere."

Leah's voice became soft as she continued to gaze at the sea. "Somewhere. A long, long time ago." She closed her eyes, hiding some inner pain, and whispered, "So very long ago."

Nathan said gently, "You aren't that old, child. Nothing can have been that long ago for you."

Leah stared at Nathan a moment, then said flatly, "I

have an old soul, Nathan Adamson. I was born old." An uncomfortable silence followed. Nathan was unsure what to do next, if anything. Finally, Leah shrugged and said, "Since Neshamah sent you, I must assume you are wanted by Adam Chata for some trespass against society as a whole. Correct?"

Nathan smiled slightly. "Something like that. I took my children to Yada rather than surrender them for government retraining."

Leah nodded knowingly. "Ah, one of those. And what did Neshamah instruct you to do once you got here?"

"Nothing. He said my responsibilities would be made clear later."

"Well, since you are here, and with no visible means of support, I suppose you should stay until someone shows up and reclaims you." Leah smiled, then motioned for Nathan to follow her. She led him to what served as a dining area. It was sparsely furnished: a small table and two chairs, pushed against the wall. Evidently Leah did not usually entertain large groups of people. Leah asked, "Are you hungry?"

"Now that you mention it, yes."

Leah said primly, "Then I shouldn't have mentioned it."

Nathan decided to adopt her bantering attitude and said, "That's what you get for asking."

"Remind me not to ask next time." The young woman gestured towards the table. "Sit. I'll fix you something."

Nathan shook his head. "I don't want to be any trouble."

"You're here, you're trouble. So? That's what life's about." Leah pointed again to the chair. "Sit. I'll be right back." She disappeared into the kitchen.

Nathan took one of the chairs and turned its back to the wall, then sank down. It was wonderful to be off his feet, finally. How long had he been going? The man tried to remember. He and the children had left Tebel-Ayr two, no, three days ago. And though it seemed like forever, it had actually been less than a full day since he'd left them with the guide. He wondered where they could be now. Along the trail, of course. The first part of Yada was easy to cross. Nathan closed his eyes and relived his own journey through Yada. Tension and weariness, anxiety and fear drained from him slowly. Nathan's head dropped onto his chest. Within moments, he was asleep.

Leah reentered the room carrying a tray of dried fruit, hard cheese, and bread. She said, "It's not much, but. . . ." The woman trailed off as she saw her guest's condition. She sighed, set the food down, and muttered, "When will you ever learn? Sleep, then food. They always fall asleep first." Bemused, she shook her head, then returned the tray to the kitchen.

Ben Ramah left the administration building and walked briskly down the street, away from the center of town. He wasn't sure where he was going; away was all he could think of. Home was out of the question; it was watched. Few places in Tebel-Ayr weren't. The presence of Adam Chata filled the queen city. The governor's likeness was displayed on every third corner. Tabbach guards lounged outside the pleasure houses. Notice boards listed where the governor would appear during the day. Working or not, people were expected to turn out to pay honor to Adam Chata.

Ben could not easily leave the capital without arousing suspicion. Not that any of the guards would dare detain him. But an extended absence might bring unwelcome attention. Somehow, having to explain his "research" to the Governor was not a scenario Ben cared to envision.

Ramah turned left at the first corner and continued walking. It would have to be some private place where he could read without interruption or fear of discovery. The penalties for possessing, much less reading, the Kathab were severe. Ben had made sure of that himself. Having all but purged its deadly influence, no one wanted to risk reinfecting society with the Kathab's intolerance, exclusivity, and guilt. The book had to be banned—for the good of all. Besides, learned men had drawn all the wisdom that was worth saving from it. Anyone that wanted to know about the Kathab could read what they had written.

Ben turned right, then left, then right again at successive intersections, wandering aimlessly through town. The streets were crowded with merchants and travelers, all with purpose and a place to go. All except Ben. He skirted a Tabbach outpost and carefully avoided the cafés he knew his students preferred.

Where could he go? The park? Too open. A reading room? That made sense, but Ben dismissed the idea. Too confining. And too many stray eyes. A friend's house, maybe? Good idea. But Ben didn't have any friends. None he'd trust with this secret, anyhow. Ben ignored the niggling voice that suggested he look up Chalaq. Too absurd. Ben continued to wander aimlessly, his frustration increasing. Where could he go? Why was this so difficult? All he wanted was a place to sit and read the Kathab.

The satchel began to grow heavier and more obtrusive at his side. Ben's imagination began to taunt him. Passersby stared at him, eyes firmly fixed on the bulging package he carried. They knew what he had. The older man on the corner, leaning against the stone carving . . . surely he was one of the secret police. He had to know Ben was carrying contraband. Ben saw—or thought he saw— the man smile knowingly, then turn and walk away. Going to notify the authorities, no doubt.

Ben doubled his pace, crossed the street quickly, and dodged between two tall buildings. A short alley led to an arcade. Ben forced himself to slow his steps and tried to mingle with the thrill seekers. But fear continued to haunt him. He watched for furtive movements, for knowing glances and telltale nods that would indicate he'd

been spotted. Years of intensive training served him well
. . . .

Or made him paranoid. Every gesture of every stranger became a signal to silent and secret observers. Ben half-imagined the entire arcade was a trap to snare him. Panic mounted in him, naked fear unlike any he'd experienced in years. And all because of a book. He should get rid of it, toss it into the nearest incinerator and be done with it. He should . . . .
Ben fled the arcade and ducked into a deserted court-yard. He was shaking uncontrollably, gasping for breath. Why? What was going on? Ben forced himself to walk to a stone table and sat down, ignoring the internal voice that urged him to run. He carefully laid the satchel down on the table and stared hard at it. He stilled the terrified chatterings inside and tried to think rationally. It was a book, just a book. Nothing more. A series of words on a page, joined together to make sentences, then para-graphs, chapters . . . a book. No book should cause this kind of reaction in him, especially one he hadn't even opened yet. But something or someone in him was death-ly afraid of the contents. Why else would he be experienc-ing such turmoil? He was acting like someone possessed
. . . .

Ben laid his hand on the satchel questioningly. He knew the Kathab was the story of the King's dealings with the 'Ibriy in history. It also told about the birth, life, and death of Haben Jah. Haben had long been claimed by the Chasidim to be the King Himself, come to His people in human form. Fairy tales, the enlightened ones insist-ed. Eyewitness accounts, the Chasidim countered. Ben wondered again at the panic he'd felt. No mere fairy tale should evoke such fear, especially in one as spiritually mature as Ben was himself. Then why was he still shak-ing? And why had all the governments from antiquity up to this day been so violently opposed to the Kathab's very existence? Ben dismissed all the propaganda he'd helped create. Those excuses were for the masses, not for people of vision.

Carefully Ben drew the small book from the satchel and stared at the cover. A voice inside vehemently urged him to throw the Kathab away. Ben ignored it. Slowly he turned the cover back. Though the Kathab wasn't thick, there were hundreds of pages. Ben thumbed through the delicate leaves gently. Where should he start looking for Neshamah?

A voice spoke quietly, "Start at the beginning."

Ben jumped up, startled and frightened. A man had approached him unawares and was standing before him. Six feet tall or so, silver hair, black eyes: a stranger. The man repeated, "Start at the beginning. Never read a story backwards."

Ben stuffed the Kathab into his satchel and said roughly, "I wasn't reading."

He made as if to leave but stopped as the man said, "Not yet. But you will. And when you do, begin in the beginning. That is where your search starts."

Ben eyed the man suspiciously, his fear growing stronger. But he covered it and demanded, "What search? I don't know what you're talking about."

The stranger held Ben's eyes momentarily; Ben was unable to look away. The man's gaze seemed to penetrate to his very soul. He said quietly, "Your search for Truth, Ben Ramah. But this is not the place to begin reading the Kathab. You are not safe here. Go to Nadiyb, nasi of Shimown. Ask after his niece; she will help you. Do not tarry here. Adam Chata is searching for you. Go quickly."

Ben stared back at the man, awed. Though he felt fear and confusion at having a stranger know so much about him and what he was doing, it did not occur to him to doubt or question what was said. The stranger spoke with an authority that was to be believed. Ben swallowed hard and asked, "Who are You? How do You know me?"

"You will come to know My name later. But I have
known you since before you were born, Ben Ramah."

"I've never seen You before."

"That is not entirely true, but that, too, will be made
clear in time. For now, do as I say. We will meet again."

Ben hesitated, questioning his own inner guide. *"What
should I do?"* But the voice had grown strangely quiet,
almost as if absent. Ben stared back into the man's eyes
and asked slowly, "How do I know this isn't a trap?"

The stranger's eyes sparkled. "In days past, when there
were still animals which roamed free, it would come to
pass that a beast would become entangled in the domin-
ions of man. It would be lost and hurt, doing harm to itself
and others. It was often necessary to trap the animal in
order to heal it and free it."

Ben's eyes narrowed. "Am I an animal?"

"No. Lost and hurt, perhaps. In need of freedom, most
definitely."

Ben said flatly, "I have total freedom. I can do anything
I want."

The man's eyes pierced Ben again and challenged him,
"Are you free from fear, Ben Ramah?"

Ben wanted to say yes, but couldn't. Part of him wanted
desperately to defy this force before him, to turn, and
walk away. But another part—a very small part, to be
sure—urged him to stay and speak the truth. Ben struggled with his answer, all the while held in the stranger's
gaze. Finally he said thickly, "No."

"Do you want to be?"

Ben closed his eyes. More a prayer than a whisper, he
answered, "Yes." Ben dropped his head and did not open
his eyes.

The stranger's voice said firmly, "Go to Nadiyb. Ask after his niece. She will help you. Go now."

Ben opened his eyes. "But how . . . ?" he stopped. There
was no one around. Ben looked quickly over the area, but
the courtyard was empty. He picked up his satchel, then

looked around one more time. Still no one. Ben started walking slowly down the street and thought, *Nadiyb of Shimown. Ask after his niece.* Suddenly Ben stopped. His eyes widened, then glimmered slightly. The face on his sketches took form and substance, and Ben whispered, "Leah."

The Search Begins

Leah sat curled up on the ledge, staring out the back window into nothingness. Evening had come; her guest was still sleeping at the dining table. The man was obviously exhausted. But, then, Neshamah's visitors usually arrived in various stages of distress.

A large orange tabby cat jumped silently onto the small ledge beside the woman and nuzzled up to her. Leah stroked him absently, without enthusiasm. She continued to stare out into the darkness. The cat bumped her hand lightly to draw her attention. Leah ignored him. She muttered softly, "He's wrong, you know. I won't shield His people forever. I can't. Sooner or later I'm going to get caught. And even Uncle Nadiyb won't be able to help me." Leah turned to eye the cat suspiciously. "Is that what He wants? Is that why He sends all these strays and stragglers here, so I will get in trouble?"

The cat ignored the question and curled up beside her. Leah shook her head. "If He's trying to force the issue it won't work. I'm not one of the Chasidim. I never have been, and I never will be. I serve the True King, not some pretender to the throne." She stared defiantly at the cat. "You tell Him that."

The cat growled softly, "You tell Him that the next time you see Him."

Leah lost her defiance as quickly as it came. "I have, Sharath. He ignores it."

The cat eyed Leah closely, staring at her with unblinking eyes. After a minute he purred, "This one bothers you. Why?"

"They all bother me, Sharath. I know how it will go. He'll spend his time here telling me how Haben Jah is the King, and how I have to accept Him as such. We'll have long discussions about what he knows and about what I know. Then he'll get mad, shake the dust from his feet, and leave. It happens every time they come. I don't need this in my life."

The cat purred, "Maybe this time it will be different."

Leah shook her head. "It's never different. I know who Haben Jah is. I like Haben Jah. I think he was a great teacher and a wonderful man. But he was a man, Sharath. Only a man. The Chasidim want to make him something more, but they're wrong."

"What if they're not?"

Leah growled back, "Don't start with me. Not tonight." The woman rubbed a hand across her face and said, "I'm supposed to go see my cousin Miriam. Uncle Nadiyb is giving her in marriage to the prime minister's son."

Sharath spat in disgust. "They should be very happy together."

Leah grinned. "Miriam and Lamech will do well. They deserve each other."

"So do their fathers."

Leah chuckled dryly. "Wouldn't that be a marriage to behold?"

"A greater union than one could imagine. The promiser and the compromiser." Sharath spat again.

Leah shuddered. "Perish the thought." She slid off her perch. "Be that as it may, I must still be polite and attend the festivities. I'll be home early, though." She hesitated, looking towards the darkened dining area. "Should I wake him first?"

Sharath stretched his front paws lazily. "I don't believe

you could. Leave him alone. I'll tell him where you have gone, if he stirs."

Leah snorted in surprise. "You'll tell him? You talk to no one but me, remember? Or so you've always claimed."

Sharath shrugged. "I can make exceptions when the need arises. I'm very versatile, you know."

"So you tell me." Leah ruffled the cat's fur briskly. "I'll see you later."

"Have fun."

Leah grimaced and crossed the room to her living quarters. What to wear? The paint smock was definitely not appropriate. Comfortable, but not appropriate. As much as she enjoyed irritating Uncle Nadiyb, tonight was not the night. Leah selected a conservative pale blue dress, added a dark blue wrap around her waist for accent, and left it at that. Jewels? No. Miriam would be wearing baubles enough for the entire assembly. Leah ran a comb quickly through her hair and headed for the door. She jerked it open, then stopped in her tracks. She stared in disbelief at the man standing before her. She lashed out, "You!"

Ben Ramah said carefully, "Good evening, Leah."

"Good evening? Good evening?" Leah was beside herself. "What are you doing here? How dare you come here, after all this time!"

Ben hesitated, then said, "I was sent here."

"By who? Your boss? My uncle? Which supreme figure of authority are you serving tonight?"

Ben cleared his throat uncomfortably. "Neither, actually. I'm here on my own . . . sort of."

Leah faked mock surprise. "Ben Ramah acting on his own? Thinking for himself? I don't believe it."

Ben glanced around behind him, then asked, "May I come in, please?"

"Please, is it? Why? What do you want here?"

Leah could tell the man was nervous, and that intrigued her. Ben Ramah had always been the epitome of grace under pressure. Nothing ever rattled him. He had been her teacher some four years ago. At least that's how it had started. What it became . . . .

Leah shook her head abruptly. "You are not welcome here, Ramah. And I was just leaving. Go away."

Ben appeared to study her, then said softly, "I guess he was wrong, then."

Leah shouldn't have asked, but couldn't help it. "Who was wrong?"

"The person who directed me here. He said you'd help me."

Leah said flatly, "You're right, he was wrong." Still, she had to know. "Who would have been foolish enough to think I'd help you?"

Ben paused, then admitted slowly, "I didn't get his name. But I think . . . ." His voice dropped, and Leah had to strain to hear him. ". . . I think it was Kadosh Neshamah. Or I thought it was. Now I'm not sure." He looked her dead in the eyes, waiting for her response.

Leah sagged against the door frame, rolled her eyes and muttered through clenched teeth, "That's it. That's it. I'm done. No more!" She glared hard at Ben and said, "Take the place, I don't care. Hide here, if that's what you're doing. Best of luck to you both." She brushed past him, leaving the door open, and walked away down the street.

Ben stared after the woman, his confusion increasing. He muttered, "Was it something I said?" He debated whether to go after her but thought better of it. Confronting an already angry woman on the street would doubtless create a commotion, and Ben was trying to avoid attention, not garner it. Ben shrugged, then stepped inside, closing the door behind him. He looked around, then announced to no one in particular, "I'm here. Now what?"

From the back room a large cat sauntered out. It took one look at Ramah, then went totally berserk. It growled, hissed, arched its back, then turned tail and ran howling from the room. Bemused, Ben shook his head. "Nice to meet you, too. I must be losing my charm. Your mistress reacted the same way." Ben dropped his satchel and walked into the back. The snoring figure at the table puzzled him. Ben studied the man closely. Something about him was familiar. Ben probed his memory but couldn't place the face. Maybe someone who looked like him, then. Say, a younger version? Ben's eyes grew wide, then hardened as the proper image finally came to view. He seethed, "Adamson. Nathan Adamson. We meet at last."

Adam Chata stared out the window of his office. Evening had fallen; the gray mist that shrouded Tebel-Ayr glowed softly with the lamps that burned throughout the city. Individual lights were indistinguishable; only the whole had any effect on the perpetual fog. The Governor turned from the window and addressed Ben Ramah's aide, "Where is Ramah? I want him brought to me."

Athariym answered nervously, "He didn't say where he was going, sir. He only said he would be gone for awhile."

Chata shook his head. "No one goes without my knowing where. I read the thoughts and hearts of men. No one can hide himself so well that I cannot discern where he is or what he is doing." Chata's eyes narrowed slightly. "But Ramah has closed himself to me, and I cannot find him. This troubles me greatly."

Athariym ventured cautiously, "He told me he was on a special assignment for you. Isn't he?"

Chata remained patient. "If I'd sent him on an assignment, I'd know where he was." Chata turned and walked to his window. He stared out thoughtfully, then said, "If he thinks to betray me, he'll find the enemy will treat him no better."

Athariym was shocked. "Ben Ramah betray you? Never! He's far too loyal to . . . ."

Chata interrupted him. "Ben Ramah's loyalty has never come into question, precisely because I know where his loyalties lie. Self-preservation is the highest cause he serves. It is that quality in him which makes him so predictable. Because of it, I can use him effectively." Adam Chata smiled. "Ramah believes he is using me for his own advancement. He has yet to see that the game is mine."

Ben's young aide shifted uncomfortably. He wondered where Ramah could have gotten to, and what he was doing to have disturbed the Governor so much. Athariym had never liked dealing directly with Adam Chata. The Governor confused and intimidated him. The aide had always found it uncanny how the man could read thoughts.

Adam Chata turned and studied the young man. He said slowly, "You, however, are interested in serving the new order, aren't you." It was not a question.

Athariym nodded. "Of course, sir. We all serve . . . ."

"Only the wise serve the True Light, Athariym. Many seek to manipulate it for their own ends yet end up working it to their destruction. Ramah is walking the thin edge between catastrophe and ruin. I have little hope of his final redemption. But you . . . ." Chata studied the man again. "You might make an excellent replacement."

Athariym swallowed hard. "I'm not worthy of your trust, sir."

Chata chuckled. "Your worth and my trust are not in question. Your willingness to serve is. Will you serve me?"

"Of course, sir. I always have."

"Very good. Find Ben Ramah. Bring him to me. Use whatever resources you need."

"But if he's hidden himself from you, how can I find him, sir?"

"He will not be expecting you to search for him. I am aware of your special talent. Report back to me when you have located him. Then go and bring him back here."

Athariym nodded. "Of course, sir. I'll do my best."

"Do better than that. Succeed." Chata smiled benevolently. "You can do all things, Athariym. There is nothing impossible for those open to the force within. Ask, and
you will receive."

Athariym nodded, warming to the idea. "Yes, Governor. I'll be back soon. Thank you."

Chata clapped the man on the shoulder, then turned
away, dismissing him.

Athariym left the office filled with pride and a new confidence. The Governor knew of his ability. Had Ben told
him? Not that it mattered how Adam Chata knew. It was
enough that he did know and now wanted Athariym to
use his talents for the new order. Finally, the chance to
exercise his gifts in service to the Governor, personally.
Simply find Ben Ramah. It would be easy, as the Governor had said. Athariym's contacts were especially adept
at locating—or creating—missing persons.

Athariym hurried to the messenger chamber: a large
pit near the back of the palace. Twenty feet in diameter,
twenty feet deep, it was the home of Adam Chata's swiftest couriers: a thousand black ravens. They could cover
the length of the city in what seemed to observers an instant, gone and back before you noticed they were gone.
The ravens were constantly on duty, freely assigned to all
who requested one. More than just messengers, the ravens also doubled as counselors, bringing the word of
Adam Chata to those in need of direction, advice, correction, or any other form of guidance. They were very popular in Tebel-Ayr; all but the Chasidim relied heavily on
their wisdom.

Athariym paced to the edge of the pit and called, "Ke-
sheph, Chartom, I need you."

Two giant ravens appeared, both with a wingspan over
eight feet. They squawked in unison, "What is your need,
Athariym?"

"Contact Kechash 'owb, Ben Ramah's messenger. Find
out where he is."

The two ravens disappeared. Athariym had just enough time to tap his foot once before the ravens reappeared. The man asked, "Well?"

Chartom squawked, his voice puzzled, "Kechash refuses to speak to us."

"Refuses? What? Why?"

"I don't know. He won't speak."

Athariym frowned. "That makes sense. But I need to speak to him. Can you take me to him?"

Chartom bobbed his head. "Of course."

The ravens launched into the air, and grabbed Athariym by his shoulders. Athariym automatically closed his eyes. While the sensation of flying was exhilarating, the actual process terrified him. The trip took several minutes; how long, Athariym couldn't be sure. Time and distance had little meaning when flying with the ravens.

Keshaph cried, "We're here."

It was a warning to Athariym to move his feet as the ravens glided him in for an awkward and uncomfortable landing. The man looked around. They were in near total darkness, in an empty field. Athariym asked, "Where are we?"

"With Kechash 'owb."

"But where is that? Where in Tebel-Ayr are we?"

"We're not in Tebel-Ayr."

Athariym suppressed a shudder. He'd never been outside the city walls before. What could Ben be doing? Athariym asked, "Where is Ben Ramah?"

"You didn't ask us that. You asked us where Kechash 'owb was."

"Because he should be with Ben!" Athariym felt his frustration rising. Unwise. Frustration blocked clear thinking. Athariym looked around him, but there was nothing to be seen. Off to his left he could barely discern a sullen grayness, and decided it must be Kechash 'owb, Ben's raven-guide. Athariym approached the bird cautiously. "Kechash, you know me. We've been friends for a long time. We've worked together, helped each other. You know you can trust me. Where is Ben Ramah?"

The raven screeched angrily but didn't answer. Athariym appealed to Chartom. "Talk to him."

"He won't talk."

"Try. It's important."

"He won't talk."

Athariym hesitated, then addressed the raven again. "Kechash, I want to know where Ben Ramah is. Can you take me there?" The raven remained silent. "Can you at least tell me why you left him?" Still the raven remained silent. Athariym coaxed, "Please, Kechash. Where is Ben? Why won't you talk even to me?"

The raven flapped its huge wings, then screeched sullenly, "I was sent away."

Athariym was shocked. "Sent away? By Ben? He'd never send . . ."

"No." Kechash's voice became even more sullen. "He doesn't even know I'm gone."

"That's impossible!" Athariym shook his head vehemently. "There is no way Ben could function without you. Who is leading him? Who sent you away?"

Kechash refused to answer. The raven turned its back on Athariym. The man repeated more strongly, "Who sent you away, Kechash? I demand you answer. By the authority of the king we serve, you must tell me. Who sent you away?"

"I DID," a powerful voice rolled across the darkness.

Shrieking, the three ravens fled, leaving Athariym alone. The man turned to face the speaker and froze. His eyes grew wide in terror. He swallowed hard twice, then fell to his knees. As full recognition set in he whispered in horror, "Oh, no. Oh, no. Ben, what have you done?"

Meetings

Leah stood silently between the mock pillars and tried to smile pleasantly. The prime minister had authorized the use of the forum for tonight's festivities because of the importance of the occasion. The marriage of the prime minister's son and Nadiyb Bataqab's daughter would unify the government and the 'Ibriy. It was a union that would ensure peace and tranquility for generations to come.

No expense had been spared to mark the occasion. Tiny lanterns strung from the ceiling resembled stars, giving an aura of divine approval to the affair. Opulence was the order of the evening; the guests had even been supplied with beautiful garments, more costume than clothing, but again, image was everything. Leah had declined to change, refusing the proffered gown and cape. The young woman's smile twisted to a snarl. She caught herself and smiled again. Happy. Pleasant, at least. For one night, she could manage to be civil.

Leah turned to watch Miriam and Lamech dance the first dance of the evening. Even the musicians had been strategically placed to enhance the mood. A narrow loft, used primarily for refilling lanterns, ran around the perimeter of the forum. Tonight the loft was occupied by a stringed octet, their heavenly strains wafting down to the crowds below. Leah shook her head and studied the couple on the floor. Neither Miriam nor Lamech ever looked at each other. Both were busily scanning the audience to see what kind of impression they were making. Leah grimaced, rolled her eyes slightly, but continued to smile. She consoled herself with the knowledge that once the general dancing started she could leave without creating a scene.

But where could she go? Home was out of the question. Not with Ramah there. Leah's smile disappeared permanently. How dare he come to her? And saying Neshamah sent him! Neshamah send Ramah anywhere? Absurd. Leah's face darkened. Of course, she couldn't deny Neshamah had sent some strange guests. But Ramah!

A man's voice disturbed her thoughts. "You look miserable. Why aren't you enjoying yourself? Jealousy, maybe?"

Leah huffed. "Of course, Daniel. I've always wanted Lamech for myself. Wasn't that obvious?"

Leah turned and hugged her older brother. He was six years her senior, and the family resemblance was striking. Daniel hugged her in return. Leah looked around, then asked, "Where is Ruth? I don't see her anywhere in your shadow."

Daniel grinned. "She is at home. The twins are not feeling well."

"Anything serious?"

"No. Colic, I'm told. Of course, I know *so much* about babies."

Leah smiled. "With six weeks experience, you should be an expert by now."

Daniel shook his head, then motioned towards the refreshment table. "Let's take advantage of Uncle Nadiyb's generous hospitality. I need something to drink."

"Sounds wonderful."

Brother and sister walked to the table. Again, Nadiyb Bataqab had spared nothing for his only daughter's engagement. The tables were laden with all the best that could be obtained—legally or otherwise—in Tebel-Ayr. Fresh breads, exotic cheeses, strange fruits of a type Leah had not seen before were piled high for all to see and enjoy.

Leah whispered, "He's outdone himself. Uncle must have raided Adam Chata's own pantries."

Daniel shrugged. "Tonight, who cares where it comes from? Enjoy. Eat, drink, and be merry. Tomorrow your conscience can bother you because you ate at the Governor's table."

Leah chuckled. "You have such a way with words, Daniel."

"Yes, don't I?" Daniel filled a crystal cup for Leah, then filled a cup for himself. They turned to watch the couple on the floor. The first dance had ended; Miriam was dancing with her father, while Lamech escorted his mother. Leah calculated the pairings and came up with four more possible interfamily combinations before the general populace would be allowed to dance, and she could make her exit. She looked at her brother. "Daniel, would it be an inconvenience if I stayed at your home tonight?"

"Of course it is. I'm surprised you would even ask."

Leah snorted. "Thank you. Your hospitality is exceeded only by your intelligence."

Daniel grinned, then asked, "Is anything wrong? You know you are always welcome to stay with us. Why tonight?"

Leah shrugged, then admitted, "It's a little crowded at my place."

"Crowded?"

"Unexpected visitors."

"Oh?" Leah nodded but did not elaborate. Daniel lowered his voice. "Neshamah sent them?"

Leah grimaced. "So they say."

Daniel appeared to study his sister, then said quietly, "If He did send them, then hiding will avail you nothing. We both know that."

Leah pleaded, "Just tonight. I promise. Please, Daniel? Just for tonight."

Daniel hesitated, then nodded. "Tonight." He said one arm protectively around his sister and added, "I've heard that special people carry special burdens."

Leah snorted, "Let someone else be special tonight."

Daniel chuckled. "Very well. Miriam and Lamech can carry the load. It is their party."

Leah grinned. "Such burdens they carry, too."

"They will."

"Amen."

The two watched silently until the last parent-grand-parent-child combination had been completed. As the general public moved out onto the parquet floor to celebrate, Daniel said, "I believe we can politely leave without disturbing anyone's sensibilities, if you care to."

Leah finished her drink and set her cup beside Daniel's. "My thoughts exactly."

"We've always thought alike." Laughing, Daniel escorted his sister out the door.

Nathan was dreaming, and it wasn't a pleasant dream. He was trapped by Adam Chata's elite guards. Everywhere he turned a soldier, armed with a flaming sword, blocked his path. They forced him down a darkened corridor to a stone prison cell. Other prisoners taunted and mocked him. Jonathan and Rachel were there, crying to him, begging him to release them from captivity. A guard pushed Nathan to the window of the cell and made him look outside. His wife, Yaldah, was standing alone in the courtyard. She was barefoot, dressed in a simple, tattered gown. Her auburn hair flowed behind her in the wind as she faced him, her eyes locked on his.

The guard prodded Nathan with his sword; the flames burned deep inside him. "Turn away from her. Turn away and you go free. Turn away."

Nathan hesitated. The guard prodded him again, ordering sharply, "Turn away! Save yourself and your children. Turn away!"

Nathan stared longingly at the silent figure in the courtyard. Then, to his horror and shame, dropped his eyes and turned away. He faced the guard and said thickly, "I denounce Yaldah and all she believes. I do not serve Haben Jah as she does. I serve only myself." Nathan stopped, then turned back to the window. The courtyard was empty: Yaldah was gone. In anguish Nathan shouted, "No! Yaldah! No!"

His own shouts woke him. Nathan jerked in the chair and knocked his head against the wall. It took him several moments to regain his bearings and shake off the nightmare images.

Yaldah had been dead fifteen years now. Could it be fifteen years? He'd made peace with his past, but the nightmares never went away completely.

Nathan looked around, remembering where he was and why. The young man that stood silently before him was a new addition to the room, though. He was studying Nathan intently, as if waiting for something. Nathan didn't know what, nor did he recognize the man. He rubbed his hand across his face, then said simply, "Bad dream. Who are you?"

The younger man's eyes narrowed as he said, "That's not important. You are Nathan Adamson, aren't you." It was an accusation, not a question.

Nathan studied the man, then said, "Yes, I am."

"Where is Jonathan?"

Nathan felt a cold chill run through him but squelched it. He prayed quickly and silently, then said, "He is on a journey."

"Where?"

Nathan countered, "How do you know my son?"

The man repeated the question. "Where did you send him?"

Nathan sat up straighter in the chair, feeling some confidence growing. "A question for a question. How do you know Jonathan?"

The man seemed to debate his options, then said, "I was his teacher."

Nathan considered this. "You mean you are his teacher. Otherwise you wouldn't know he was gone."

"Shrewd." The younger man nodded, awarding the first point to Nathan. "I see Jon came by his mental agility honestly." Nathan's adversary sat down at the table and faced Nathan. "Yes, I am his teacher. Where did you take him?"

"To safety."

"Where?"

Nathan arched one eye. "Are we naming names? I didn't catch yours."

The man snorted. "I thought honesty was the first law of the Chasidim."

Nathan quoted, " 'Wise as serpents, harmless as doves.' Serving Haben Jah doesn't strip a man of his intellect. It gives him a new one, in fact."

"Uh huh." Nathan read the disgust in the man's tone. But the younger man did not challenge the response. He studied the patterns in the wood grain of the table, then admitted, "I am Ben Ramah." He looked directly at Nathan and waited.

Nathan's eyes narrowed, and his jaws tightened visibly. But he held his immediate response in check. It took a moment, but he nodded. "I see." Nathan drew a deep breath, let it out slowly, then said, "I took Jonathan to Yada, along with his sister Rachel."

To Nathan's surprise Ben merely nodded. "I see."

There was a long silence. Finally Nathan asked, "How did you know I was here?"

"I didn't."

"You didn't come here looking for me?"

"No."

"I see."

Another long silence followed. Nathan looked around. "Where is Leah?"

Nathan noted a quick flash of guilt in Ben's eyes, but the younger man said only, "She left. She did say we had the place at our disposal, though." Ben asked, "How do you know Leah Bataqab?"

"I don't. Or I didn't, before today."

"Then why are you here?"

Nathan hesitated. "A friend sent me." No sense implicating the woman in his crimes.

"A friend? A friend of Leah's?"

How to answer that one? Nathan pondered. Finally he said, "I don't know. Possibly." Nathan countered, "How do you come to be here?"

Again Nathan caught the momentary flicker in Ben's eyes. "Leah and I were friends, once. I was her teacher."

"Which answers how you know her, not why you are here." Ben remained silent. Nathan added, "You didn't come to renew old acquaintances."

Ben eyed Nathan, calculating. He admitted, "No. I was directed here."

"By a friend?"

"Not exactly."

Nathan smiled inwardly as he guessed the identity of Ben's director. He thought, *Not exactly? I'll bet!* Aloud he said, "I see."

Ben snarled, "Neither of us sees anything, so let's dispense with the games. Kadosh Neshamah sent me here, the same as He did you. Why?"

"He didn't say, and I didn't ask." Not exactly true, but close enough. Nathan continued, " 'Why' is not a word Neshamah chooses to respond to, as a rule."

"So I've heard. But you Chasidim are supposed to know Him, to have His mind, so you say. Doesn't that give you special insight?"

Nathan was aware of a subtle change in Ben's questioning. The sarcasm was still present, but he sensed an underlying desire for real answers. Nathan considered the question, then said, "Sometimes. Not always. In a given situation He may choose to reveal that portion of His mind that concerns us. Usually we respond by faith."

Ben objected in disgust. "Faith? In what? Provision for well being? Security in times of peril? Physical safety? Health and prosperity? What is it you have faith for? The Chasidim are the most persecuted, downtrodden, deprived group of people in existence today."

Nathan said dryly, "You ought to know. You orchestrated most of it."

Ben ignored the remark. "You didn't answer my question. Faith in what?"

Nathan was silent a long time, trying to decide how to answer. Ben watched impatiently, then demanded, "Faith in what? You don't know, do you?"

Nathan eyed Ben. "Why does it matter to you?"

"Just tell me the answer!" Ben rose abruptly from the table and paced back and forth in the small kitchen. "What is it that drives you people? I don't understand. I've never understood. I see the Chasidim lose their houses, their property, their privileges, their rights . . . ." Ben stopped his pacing and looked intently at Nathan. "Why? For what? Tell me."

"You really want to know, don't you?"

"Yeah, I really want to know."

Nathan prayed quickly, "Lord King, direct my words." A passage from the Kathab came to him: *"In the day you are brought before the judges, don't worry about what you will say. It will be given to you."* Nathan half-nodded and said silently, *"Then give it now, Lord."* He said, "We have faith in Haben Jah. Faith in Who He is, and what He says."

Ben stared back at Nathan. "Haben Jah. A man who

died how many thousands of years ago, if he even lived at all."

Nathan nodded. "He lived. He lives now."

"How do you know that? How is it you are so sure you will bet your life and everything else on it?"

"We have His Word, and we have His Spirit."

Ben sat down but continued to challenge Nathan's answers. "His Word. You mean the Kathab, right?"

"Right."

"You base everything you believe on a fairy tale."

Nathan asked, "What do you base your beliefs on?"

Ben shook his head. "That's not the issue."

"Yes it is. You asked me what I believe, and why. I told you. Now, you tell me. What do you believe in, and why?"

There was a long silence as Ben searched for an answer. He'd never thought about it before. And now that he'd been challenged, he didn't know what to say. Nathan Adamson sat across from him, without fear, without malice, waiting for his answer. Ben studied the table top, marshaling his thoughts. The pat answers no longer seemed to serve. *"I believe in what I see and feel . . . ."* Yet all of life, especially in Adam Chata's world was predicated on creating that which wasn't there, rather than being limited by that which was. *"I believe in myself."* Also invalid. The most fundamental challenge of all was the debate, *"Prove you exist."* Ben grew increasingly uncomfortable under Nathan's even gaze. *"I believe in Adam Chata."* Not a belief system guaranteed to bring peace and happiness. Certainly not one he was willing to lose his life for. Finally, after five minutes of silence he admitted, "I don't know." He looked at Nathan. "I don't know."

There was a twinkle in the man's eyes, and Ben thought he saw the slightest trace of a cold smile. But Nathan only nodded. "I see. I see."

6

Shadows

Athariym stood outside the Governor's private chambers, drew himself up, and knocked strongly on the door. He straightened his tunic and waited. Adam Chata called out sharply, "Come." Athariym stepped inside and faced the Governor.

Adam Chata was seated in front of the windows, looking out over the pre-dawn fog. He smiled as Athariym approached and said gravely, "You've found Ben Ramah."

Athariym risked one furtive look around the room; he'd never been inside the Governor's study before. One wall was ceiling-to-floor shelves, crammed full of books. The ceiling was twelve feet high and the wall twenty feet long. He'd never seen so many books. Athariym briefly wondered if the Governor had indeed read them all. Or had read any of them. The third wall was partially covered with the rich tapestries the Governor so loved. The curtains were pulled slightly open. A bench by the windows provided a cozy nook for gazing out over the city. Or what you could see of it through the fog. The perpetual, dreary fog . . . .

Athariym straightened his tunic again and faced the Governor. He'd rehearsed his answer carefully during his long walk back to the city and through a sleepless night. He repeated it diligently. "Sir, Ben Ramah has been intercepted by the enemy. My sources have narrowed his location to one of three possible areas within the city. I believe we can isolate it even further inside the next few hours. I believe Ben is being held against his will. The enemy is attempting to force him to commit treason. But I also believe they will be unsuccessful. Ben Ramah is too strong for them. He would never betray you or the new order." Athariym nearly sighed with satisfaction but refrained from outward demonstrations. He studied the governor to see what effect his speech was having.

Adam Chata never lost his patient smile. He took the news silently, waited for Athariym to finish, then nodded. "So. You believe all that, do you?"

"Yes, sir. My sources inform me Ben is currently being detained either near the Bavith, near old town, or over on the south side of Tebel-Ayr." Athariym added quickly, "I realize those are highly divergent areas, sir, and all nonspecific. But the search is continuing at this hour. I believe I will have his exact whereabouts pinpointed by tonight at the latest."

"You believe."

"Yes, sir."

Adam Chata eyed Athariym closely. "You have until sunrise tomorrow for your beliefs to bear fruit, Athariym. Faith without works is dead." Chata paused, then repeated, "Dead. Do you understand?"

Athariym nodded. "Yes, sir, I do. I'll find him, sir. I will."

"Good. See me again tomorrow. With Ramah."

Chata looked away from Athariym, dismissing him. The younger man turned and walked deliberately from the room, stilling the panic inside. Tomorrow—twenty-four hours. Plenty of time—he hoped. Athariym closed the door carefully behind him.

Leah stretched uncomfortably on her brother's couch, rubbing a hand sleepily across her face. The twins had roused the household early and often. Whoever invented the expression "sleep like a baby" hadn't had children. Leah yawned, sat up, then looked around. Daniel's home was only slightly larger than her own, yet four people . . . well, two big people and two little people . . . lived there. Leah smiled. Baby things seemed to dominate the house. Stuffed animals, wooden pull toys, blocks, diapers drying on a line strung over the wood stove . . . Who really ruled here? Leah shook her head. This was not the life for her. Not yet, anyhow. Someday. Maybe.

Leah rose quietly, wrapped a wool blanket around her, and walked to the kitchen area. A small patio filled with clay pots and planters opened off the back entrance, Ruth's garden. Through a valiant attempt on her part, and to her credit, a few hardy plants actually grew. Herbs, mostly, and some succulents. More decorative than functional, but Leah knew their purpose. Her sister-in-law was as opposed to the new order as Leah was herself. But where Leah painted, Ruth gardened. Futile protests, perhaps, but protests all the same.

And speaking of protests, it was time she voiced a few of her own. Daniel had made it clear last evening that while Leah was welcome to spend the night, she had to return home today. Daniel was always an advocate of facing one's problems. Leah frowned. She whispered, "Fine, *you* face them. I'd rather stay here until they go away."

From the back bedroom the piercing wails of an infant split the silence. Leah grinned and shook her head. "Then again, at least you can reason with adults." She sighed. Not that Ben Ramah was an adult. An overgrown weasel, a serpent in snake's clothing, perhaps, but not an adult. Leah grimaced. Once again she thought angrily, *How dare he come to me!* And saying Neshamah sent him. Neshamah send Ben Ramah? Impossible. The very idea was unthinkable.

Leah curled up on a bench between two planters. She saw no signs of life. If there were seeds below, she couldn't tell. She heard Ruth trying to comfort the ailing infant, shushing and cooing to him. Her efforts were only partially effective. One voice ceased crying, and another began. Motherhood. Leah shuddered.

But what of Nathan Adamson? She'd been wrong to run out on him, leaving him to face Ramah. Especially if he was wanted by Adam Chata. Then again, she hadn't invited him, either. Kadosh Neshamah had sent him. If there was a conflict of timing, it was Neshamah's problem, not hers. Let Him sort it out. Right?

Wrong. Leah ground her teeth in frustration. She'd agreed long ago to help the Chasidim all she could, anyway she could. Not because she believed in Haben Jah, but because the Chasidim had . . . .

Leah let the thought trail off. She whispered softly, "You were wrong, you know. I love you both, and I'll always miss you, but you were wrong." If ever she saw her parents again, that's what she would say. After she hugged them and kissed them and told them how much she'd missed them these past fifteen years. Fifteen years, six months, twenty-two days . . . .

Leah shook her head again. It was too early in the morning for such thoughts. And it didn't change the crisis at her house. The Chasidim had tried to help her parents, and she was honor-bound to help the Chasidim in return. She had an obligation to Nathan Adamson, stranger though he might be. She would have to go back and salvage whatever was left. Not a pretty thought. But, then, few of hers were these days. Leah wrapped the blanket around her more tightly and nodded to herself. "I'll go. I won't like it, but I'll go." She peered around surreptitiously and repeated to no one in particular, "Do you hear? I'll go."

If she expected thunderclaps or some other demonstration of divine approval, she didn't get any. There was a very small sense deep in her heart that she was right, but it did little to encourage her. The twins were finally silent again. Leah guessed Ruth had gone back to bed. Carefully folding her blanket, the young woman decided not to wait until daylight to go home. Leah laid the blanket neatly on a chair, scribbled a brief note to Daniel, then quietly let herself out the front door. Her brother would understand. Daniel understood most things. He'd always been her pillar of strength and comfort, especially in the years following their parents' disappearance.

Leah frowned as she walked through the silent columns of houses. She passed row upon row of sandstone and lime dwellings, all alike in form and fashion. Her thoughts kept drifting back to her parents, and she didn't know why. It was an old issue, long settled, resolved, forgotten . . . .

Not forgotten. Not resolved, either. But settled. She'd been ten years old when Hannah and Samuel Bataqab had betrayed their family and their faith, and had chosen to serve Haben Jah. Taking Daniel and Leah, they crossed Yada to Amanah, home of the King. It was there Leah first saw Haben Jah and heard of Kadosh Neshahmah.

Leah's frown softened slightly as she walked, remembering Haben Jah. She'd been as taken with Him as any other follower of His ever was. His love, kindness, gentleness, peace . . . how could anyone not follow the Man? Along with Daniel she made a pledge to follow Him, as her parents had. And it seemed right and real and beautiful when it happened.

Leah whispered, "Because I was ten and didn't know better. Uncle Nadiyb took care of that, though."

Dark memories played back in her head. Samuel had answered his brother's summons; the two men stood in the front room of Nadiyb's home. Leah had followed her father against orders and crouched in hiding outside the door to see what would happen. Nadiyb thundered furiously, "You went where?"

"Amanah."

"Never! No Bataqab leaves the fold! How dare you disgrace our family! Daniel is the last of our seed, the sole heir to the promise. You cannot take him from the faith. I will not allow it!" Nadiyb's eyes burned with fury. He bellowed fiercely, "Destroy yourself if you choose; I'll even help you. But you will not take Daniel with you!"

Leah's father spoke calmly, "The boy has made his own decision, Nadiyb."

"No, he has not. He knows nothing of what it means to be truly 'Ibriy. You have failed him in that. I will not allow you to fail him again. He will not leave the tribe."

"He has already left, Brother."

"Never!" Incensed, Nadiyb swung wildly and knocked Samuel to the floor. Leah crouched lower behind the door, afraid to stay, more afraid to run. She saw blood on her father's face as he stood up silently. Nadiyb swung again, knocking Samuel down a second time. He bellowed, "You are no Bataqab. Never again! Get out of my house. Get out of my life! Filth! Vermin! Out!"

Leah whimpered painfully, "Daddy," but was helpless to do anything. She watched her father climb to his feet again and stand before his brother one last time. Samuel wiped the blood from his mouth, looked at his hand, then looked back to Nadiyb. He said quietly, "Haben Jah had His blood spilt, too."

Nadiyb grabbed Samuel and fiercely thrust him out the door. "Go! Never come back! Leave!" Samuel caught his balance and walked purposefully away. He did not turn back. Samuel crossed the street and disappeared from view.

Leah turned onto her own street then stopped, waiting for the shadows to recede, as was their custom. But this morning they wouldn't. The specters were determined to relive the entire saga in spite of her. Leah shook her head slightly. No use in fighting them. Play it out and be done with it. Leah had been too scared then to return home immediately, afraid Samuel would know she'd followed him. Instead she went to the Bavith. Behind the sanctuary was a play area for the younger children, designed to entertain the little ones while the adults conducted their affairs for the King. Caretakers were always on duty; Leah recognized Miriam, her cousin. The thirteen-year-old was on duty and smiled as Leah came in. Five rambunctious toddlers clung to her skirts, demanding attention. Miriam called, "Leah, thank goodness you're here! Help me entertain this crowd, will you?"

Leah nodded gratefully, scooped up the youngest of the brood and cuddled the squirming boy. Miriam asked, "What brings you here today? Are your mother and father here, too?"

Leah shook her head and said shakily, "No, they're at home. My father has to work the quarry this evening. I thought I'd leave him to get some rest."

Miriam bought the lie without question. "I'm glad you're here." The teenager studied Leah a moment, then asked in a low whisper. "Is it true you really did go to Amanah? And met Haben Jah?"

Leah sighed, "Please, Miriam, not you, too. I don't want to talk about it now. Please?"

Miriam shrugged. "Suit yourself. I'm just curious, that's all. I'll bet my father gets upset, though. You know how he feels about all that."

Leah said hastily, "Change the subject, Miriam, please? Talk about something else. How is Lamech?"

Miriam blushed and Leah knew she'd scored a direct hit on her cousin. The older girl smiled and her eyes sparkled. "Oh, that one. Fine. Just fine."

Leah kept her cousin talking until her shift ended. Just before evening prayers Leah decided it would be safe to return home. She'd told the truth about her father working the quarry. She knew he would be gone before she got there.

He was. Leah entered their small dwelling cautiously

and looked around. Hannah sat alone at the table sewing a brightly colored smock. She glanced up as Leah passed her and said, "You're late. Where have you been? Your father missed seeing you before he left."

Leah refused to look at her mother but said hastily, "I worked at the Bavith with Miriam. I'm sorry. I have to work on my studies." The girl didn't wait for an answer, but disappeared quickly into her room. She shut the door tightly and leaned against it. She half expected her mother's knock, but none came. Apparently she was to be left alone with her excuse. Leah sighed, moved to her bed and sat down. She picked up the book she'd been reading the night before and started reading.

The remainder of the evening passed quietly. Hannah brought Leah a tray of food but otherwise left her undisturbed. It was unusual for her mother to be so uninquisitive, but tonight Leah preferred it that way. She read until past her bedtime, then reluctantly put her book away and crawled into bed. Tomorrow would be better. It would be.

Hannah came in quietly and tucked her daughter in, kissing the girl lightly. "Sleep well, Leah."

There was pain in Hannah's eyes, and it frightened Leah. Something was wrong. Mother knew it, too. Yet Leah could not bring herself to ask. Tomorrow. They'd set it all straight tomorrow, and then they could resume their lives as before. Hannah turned down the lamp and left the room silently. Leah closed her eyes and shut it all out. In moments she was asleep.

It was near midnight when a banging on the door woke her. She sat upright in her bed and strained to hear what was happening. Distraught voices demanded attention and admission. Leah caught a few words: accident . . . injury . . . danger . . . But who or what remained unclear. Leah cried out sharply "Mother! Mother!" Panic and fear gripped her, though she did not know why.

Hannah rushed into Leah's room hurriedly and gathered her frightened daughter into her arms. Leah clung tightly to her and demanded, "What is it? What's wrong?"

Hannah rocked her gently and said, "I'm not sure, Leah. Something has happened at the quarry. Your aunt is here; she says I'm wanted."

"Wanted? Wanted by who? Is Daddy OK?" Leah began to cry, her fear mounting.

Hannah shushed her soothingly, "Daddy serves Haben Jah, Leah. Haben will watch over him, no matter what. I've got to go. Your aunt will stay with you and Daniel until I get back. Try to go back to sleep. I'll see you in the morning." She kissed Leah lightly, then waited for her daughter to release her.

Leah calmed down slightly, reassured by her mother's confidence. "If you say so."

"I do." Hannah smiled. "Better?"

Leah nodded, releasing her mother. "Better. Wake me up when you get back, please."

"I will." Hannah kissed Leah lightly again, and waited until the girl settled back under her covers. She rose from the bed, smiled one last time, then turned and was gone.

Leah turned the last corner to home, her face drawn and resigned. No tears came, she'd cried them all years ago. Neither of her parents had returned that night. Morning had come and gone. Leah and Daniel attended school as usual, as if nothing was wrong. But when they returned home, home was gone. The house had been stripped bare. Only the children's belongings remained, packed in crates and ready to be moved. Nadiyb supervised a work crew that loaded the last of the boxes onto a cart.

Daniel put an arm protectively around his sister and approached the men. He demanded, "What are you doing? Where are you taking all this?"

Nadiyb's face was hard and cold. His voice carried no

threat but brooked no argument. "Your parents are gone. You are to come live with me."

Leah began shaking; Daniel's voice quavered "Gone? Gone where?"

"Gone." Nadiyb's eyes flared slightly, but he did not elaborate. He motioned for the workmen to finish the loading, then addressed the children again. "I am your guardian. You will come with me and stay."

Daniel ignored the statement and demanded again, "Where are Mother and Father? What has happened to them?"

"Come with me."

Leah cried out, "No!"

Daniel insisted, "We're not going anywhere until you tell us what happened to Mother and Father. Where are they?"

Nadiyb looked at both children with an icy glare and said coldly, "Were you not taught to honor and respect the leader of your people? Not even your father would teach you to disobey me. I have said what I have said. Follow me, now."

Leah and Daniel exchanged glances; Leah waited for Daniel to decide. After a moment he nodded shakily. "For now. We'll come with you for now. But only until we find out what happened to our parents. I swear by the King, we will find out."

Nadiyb remained unimpressed. "Be not hasty to vow before the Lord your God. Many a fool has been snared by the words of his mouth. Now come."

Reluctantly Daniel and Leah followed Nadiyb down the street.

They never found out what had happened that night. Every query, every attempt to discover the truth was met with dissimulation and censure. For years Leah and Daniel fought to break the conspiracy of silence, to no avail. Samuel and Hannah were gone. Not dead, gone. There were no bodies or explanations of what happened.

"Gone" required nothing, gave nothing. And nothing was all they ever found.

Leah sighed deeply then whispered to no one, "I love you." She drew a deep breath, stared at the door in front of her and muttered, "Now, back into the fire. I sure hope You know what You're doing." She opened the door and stepped inside.

The Heart of the Matter

Athariym sat quietly at Ben Ramah's desk, resting his hand lightly on the top. Perhaps physical contact with his quarry's possessions would bring inspiration. The messages in front of him brought no encouragement. Four more reports of Ramah sightings, all from opposite corners of the city. Either Ben was everywhere or nowhere. The most adept of Athariym's contacts had been unable to isolate Ramah's position, other than "somewhere inside the city." That wasn't good enough.

Athariym pushed his chair back from the desk and sighed deeply. There had to be a way to find Ramah. No one disappeared completely. But Ben's trail had ended near the arcade, when Kechash 'owb had been sent away.

Athariym shifted uncomfortably in his chair. The encounter with the ravens still haunted him. The idea that Kadosh Neshamah had somehow captured Ben was absurd. Yet there was no denying His presence or His authority to banish Kechash from Ben's life.

Athariym rolled the unpleasant thoughts in his mind, then stopped. Maybe he'd been approaching this from the wrong angle. If Ben had somehow become involved with the Chasidim, then they needed to be questioned. Perhaps Athariym could force the issue and either draw Ramah out of hiding or effect his return. But he had to act quickly; three precious hours had already slipped away. Athariym would not face Adam Chata alone and empty-handed. The young man rose abruptly and walked rapidly to the door. He caught the guard on duty and ordered urgently, "Return to your headquarters. Tell your chief I want five prominent Chasidim leaders brought in for questioning. I don't care which ones, and I want this as public a display as possible. Tell your chief Ben Ramah is missing, and the Chasidim are behind his disappearance. He has one hour to bring the men to me. Do you understand?"

The guard nodded, then asked, "On whose authority do I place these demands?"

Athariym hesitated, then said, "On Adam Chata himself."

"As you say, sir. I'll tell him." The guard saluted, then sprinted away down the hall.

Athariym watched the man go then turned back to the office. He muttered, "I will *not* face Chata alone."

Nathan and Ben faced each other across the small table, as they had throughout the long night. Half-empty cups of now-cold coffee sat untouched between them. Both men were exhausted, but neither was willing to withdraw from the battlefield or even request a ceasefire. Yet as the night had progressed to morning, the accusations and counteraccusations, malice and suspicion, had been worn down until they were reduced to mere questions and answers. Understanding what the answers meant would have to wait for clearer heads. If they could find them again.

Nathan stretched uncomfortably and asked, "Do you want more coffee?"

Ben grimaced. "No. I don't see why you drink this stuff. It tastes terrible and it poisons your body."

Nathan grinned. "All part of its charm. It keeps you awake, more than anything else."

Ben sighed slightly, then pushed his cup forward. "Then give me more."

"You don't have to stay up, you know. We could continue this after we both got some sleep."

"Not a chance," Ben shook his head sharply. "Give you the opportunity to rethink your answers? To call in reinforcements? I think not."

Nathan shrugged. "I've been calling on reinforcements all night. Or hadn't you noticed."

Ben frowned. "I noticed, I noticed." He stared at the table top reflectively, then said quietly, "So the heart of the matter is Haben Jah."

"The heart of the matter is Haben Jah."

Ben looked up at Nathan "I still don't understand. It still sounds too easy, too simplistic. He died, then came back, so you could be forgiven. Forgiven of what? You still haven't convinced me that the entire world is under some sort of curse."

"It isn't my job to convince you, Ramah."

Ben's eyes arched. "Oh? Then what have we been doing all night? Waltzing?"

Nathan shrugged. "I didn't say I wouldn't try. But I'm supposed to know it's not my job."

"Then whose job is it?"

"Kadosh Neshamah's."

Ben took this silently. The idea of facing Neshamah again was daunting, so he ignored it for the moment. "And what is your job?"

"To share the truth. You've heard it, now you're responsible for it."

"Hmmm." Ben chewed on that a moment, then asked "And if I hadn't heard, I wouldn't be responsible?"

Nathan shook his head. "I'm not getting into that."

"Why not?"

"Because it's beyond me, that's why. I'll stick to talking of what I know. I never claimed to have *all* the answers. I know what I know, and that's sufficient. If the time comes I must understand more, Neshamah will tell me."

"Just like that. You need an answer, He gives it to you. Poof! Instant wisdom."

Nathan said wearily, "No, not like that. We went over that before. Each of us is responsible to learn as much as we can about the King, Haben Jah, and Neshamah. That's why we have the Kathab: to teach us what to do, what to say, how to act and react. That's part of our job. You can't share truth if you don't know it."

"Then why do you need Neshamah?"

Nathan countered, "Why do your students need you? Or do you just give them the textbook and say 'go learn it on your own'?"

Ben pondered this, then shook his head "But . . . ."

Nathan threw up an hand. "Enough. No more buts. Class dismissed." He looked at Ben. "Argument and discussion will not win anyone to Haben Jah. You meet Him by faith or not at all. Neshamah will reveal that to you, if you let Him. If you are truly seeking Haben Jah, He will guide you."

Ben's face darkened. "I never said I wanted to find Haben Jah. I'm just trying to figure out what motivates you people. And I still don't understand it."

"Then let it go for now."

"I can't." Ben stared at the table, unwilling to look at Nathan. "I can't."

"Why?" Ben didn't answer. Nathan studied the man a moment, then asked, "Why did you come here? Aside from Neshamah's leading, why are you outside your ivory tower, asking all these questions? You and your Governor had all that settled, didn't you? We're all serving the same King. Haben Jah was a myth, Neshamah is a figment of the Chasidim's imagination, and the Kathab no longer exists. Isn't that the master plan?"

Ben continued to stare at the table, fingering the cup before him. He was silent a moment, then said slowly, "Something like that."

"What went wrong?"

Ben looked up. "You. The Chasidim. No other faction in the world refuses to accept or at least cooperate with the master plan. I thought you were just crazy. But it's more than that. I want to know what."

"To know what is to know Who. Only Haben Jah can change a man from the inside."

Ben shook his head "I've seen men changed before. Adam Chata changes people all the time."

"Do they stay changed? Or have they merely exchanged one vice for another?"

Before Ben could answer, the front door opened. Both men looked up, startled and uneasy. Leah walked in quietly and surveyed the table. Nathan smiled; Ben did not. Leah said evenly, "I see you found the coffee. Is there any left?" She addressed her comments to Nathan, purposefully ignoring Ramah.

Nathan nodded. "It's probably too strong; it's been brewing most of the night."

"I see." Leah didn't expand on the comment but went to the kitchen and poured herself a cup. Her "guests" were still present. Leah knew she'd have to force herself to be civil to Ramah. *That snake . . . .*

Leah shut off the thought quickly. This was not the time. Pleasant. Controlled, at least. Calm. That was what was required. Self-control. Discipline. Murder . . . .

Leah sighed and took her cup back to the dining area. Nathan offered her his chair, but she refused. "I'll stand."

"Where did you go last night?" Nathan asked. "I didn't mean to run you out of your home."

"I had a previous commitment." Leah tasted the coffee, then grimaced. "This is awful."

Nathan nodded. "I warned you." He stood up. "I'll make a fresh pot."

"I won't be staying. I've got to go to work." Leah couldn't resist the jab. "Unlike some, I don't have a wealthy benefactor supporting me."

Nathan chuckled. "Some of us are more fortunate than

others, I suppose. Perhaps one day I will be able to repay your hospitality."

Leah shook her head. "That wasn't what I meant." She set the cup on the table and added, "Nor who I meant, either." Without another word she turned and walked out.

Ben looked at Nathan. "She was referring to me."

"I gathered that. But 'a soft answer turns away wrath.' No sense starting arguments this morning."

Ben snorted "Right. We haven't settled the first one we started."

Nathan stretched uncomfortably, then asked, "Won't you be missed today?"

"No. I told my aide I'd be out awhile. He knows better than to look for me." Ben eyed Nathan curiously. "What about you?"

"I'm already missing. And wanted."

"So what are you going to do?"

"Wait for instructions."

"How long?"

"Until they come."

"What if they don't?"

"They will."

"But what if they don't? Then what?"

"I was given one set of instructions to follow: come here and wait. I'll follow those instructions until others are given."

"But what . . . ?"

Nathan shook his head. "There are no buts. When Haben says wait, I wait."

Ben couldn't disguise the disgust in his voice. "You make it so simple."

"It is. I trust Him. He gave me a clear command, and I'm to obey it."

"Blind obedience."

"Whom do you obey?"

Ben shook his head. "No one."

"Oh?"

Ben backed off. "All right, my superiors."

"Sometimes. And yourself, right?"

Ben thought a moment. "Myself. I'm a free man; this is a free society."

"Free from everything but fear. Your freedom is a lie, Ben Ramah. The only true freedom is in service to the King. When He makes you free, then you'll be truly free."

Ben said darkly "We covered this before."

"I know."

There was a long pause, then Ben said slowly, "But what about . . . ?"

Leah closed the door to her bedroom firmly, then dropped down on the corner of her bed. Rehashing the past left her emotionally drained. Facing Ben again was more than she cared to deal with right now. The excuse about work was convenient, if not entirely true. Painting was her livelihood; that, and the stipend from Uncle Nadiyb. Blood money, of course, but Leah took it. Nadiyb had always provided well for his brother's children, at least monetarily. But while she might take his money, Leah fiercely maintained her independence from his control.

Leah stood up slowly. She'd go work at the Bavith. There was always something that needed to be done. Today, anything was preferable to staying home. And it wasn't hiding. Adamson and Ramah seemed to be doing fine without her. It wasn't her they needed, just her house. Besides, if she was out among the people, she'd know more of what was going on. Ramah's coming was suspicious. Ramah himself was suspicious. But coming here. . . . That was a bit excessive, even for him. Something must be wrong. Not for one minute did she believe his line about, "Neshamah sent me." Adam Chata had to be behind this. It was a plot, that's all. A plot against her?

Leah dismissed the idea. If Chata wanted her, he had enough violations on file to put her away permanently. But she was too insignificant for the Governor to be bothered with. Besides, Adam Chata still needed the goodwill of the 'Ibriy for the city to function well. He would not risk offending the most influential 'Ibriy leader by arresting his niece. And sending Ramah was too elaborate. No, the plot must be against Adamson and the Chasidim. Therefore, if Leah truly wanted to help, she would be out, watching and listening. Right. It made good sense to her. Perfect sense. She'd do it. She'd do anything but stay here and deal with Ramah.

Leah stood up abruptly and moved to her closet. She changed quickly, combed her hair, then walked back into the dining area.

Ben and Nathan were still seated at the table, lost in debate. Nathan looked up as she entered, started to stand, but Leah waved him off. She noticed Ben would not meet her eyes, even now. The young woman announced, "I'm working at the Bavith. I'll be back late this evening. I suppose I'll see you then, unless your Guide moves you elsewhere."

Nathan shrugged. "Could be. I appreciate your hospitality. I will pay you back."

"No you won't. But someone else may. Just be careful." Turning on her heel, she left the house.

Ben waited until Leah was gone, then looked up. He noted the questioning look in Nathan's eyes, but would not answer. He deflected the inquiry and asked, "How did you know it was time to take Jonathan and Rachel away?"

"Neshamah told me."

"Just like that. Out of nowhere Neshamah pops up and says, 'Go.' "

Nathan thought, then nodded. "Something like that. Sometimes that's what happens. Other times, He speaks through the Word."

"The Word. The Kathab. How can something written however many years ago have meaning to you?" Ben's frustration was still obvious. "This book wasn't written to you, or about you. It was written to a select group of wandering 'Ibriy that tried to make a superstition into fact and failed."

Nathan studied Ben for a long time, then said slowly, "Until you read it for yourself, you'll never understand. Read it and find out."

Ben shook his head. "I know people who have read this thing, and they aren't flaming fanatics. Learned men have . . . ."

Nathan cut him off. "Learned men, professing themselves to be wise, have become fools. You want to know the Truth? Ask. Ask Neshamah to guide you to Him. Look for Haben Jah in all the pages; He's there. Cover to cover, first page to last, He's there. And you are there too. You, Ben Ramah, personally addressed and accounted for. Ask Neshamah. He will show you. But you have to ask, first."

Ben fingered the book lying on the table between them, then said softly, "All that in these little pages. Hard to believe."

"Until you read it."

Ben shrugged. "So you say." He drew a long breath, let it out slowly, then stretched uncomfortably. "I could use something to eat. What about you?"

"I agree."

Ben stood up. "We'll call a truce. I'll fix breakfast . . . ." He looked outside, then nodded, ". . . it is still breakfast. After, maybe I'll have a few more questions."

Nathan smiled wryly. "I'm sure you will."

The next hour passed quietly, though. Ben couldn't think of any questions for which the answer wouldn't be, "read the Kathab," so he didn't ask. The two men made a breakfast of dried fruit and toast. Nathan offered again to make more coffee, but Ben declined hurriedly. Enough was enough. And if coffee was a mainstay of the Chasidim, Ben wasn't sure he had the stomach for it.

As they silently washed up the few dishes and cups, motion at the back window caught Ben's eye. A large orange cat was scratching impatiently at the glass. Nathan looked at Ben questioningly. Ben shrugged "Must be Leah's; I saw it last night, briefly." He thought, *Very briefly*.

Nathan opened the window. The cat jumped inside. It bristled as it passed Ramah, but otherwise ignored him. The cat walked to the center of the room and sat down, staring at the two men. Nathan glanced at Ben and chuckled, "We're being watched."

The cat growled slightly, then spoke. Ben jumped in surprise. Nathan merely turned and listened. The cat said, "I have a message from Kadosh Neshamah. You are in danger here and must leave. Adam Chata is searching for you and will determine your whereabouts shortly. Be prepared to move quickly. You'll be directed where to go when the time comes." Having delivered his pronouncement, the cat stood up and strode purposefully from the room.

Ramah's eyes widened in disbelief. He looked at Nathan and asked, "What?"

Nathan said, "We're in danger. You already knew that, though."

Ben shook his head. "The cat . . . it spoke. It talked. Cat's can't do that."

"This one did."

"But . . . ." Ben floundered for words but found none. He stared after the cat, then turned to Nathan. "What do we do now?"

Nathan sighed ever so slightly. "*We* do nothing. *I* wait here. You are a free agent, remember? What you do is up to you."

Abruptly, Leah burst through the front door, her face flushed. She'd obviously been running. "Did Sharath

Shinan give you the message?" She bent over, hands on her knees, trying to catch her breath.

Ben asked, "Who?"

"Sharath Shinan. My cat. He told me we are in danger.

Nathan nodded, remaining calm. "He told us."

Leah eyed Ben coldly. "It's you, isn't it? You brought this on me."

Ben shook his head. "I had nothing to do with it. Adamson is the one they want, not me." Half-truth. The wrong half, but who knew?

Nathan said quietly, "Harboring me is a risk. I didn't expect this to happen so quickly, but there it is."

Leah said flatly, "It's not you, it's him. I know it is." She glared icily at Ben. "You have been the center of trouble in my life for years. I don't want you here. Get out."

Ben started to move; Nathan waved him back. "Listen to me, both of you." His voice was sharp with authority. "Calm down and think. The instruction was to wait, to be prepared to move, not to move on our own. Running off on our own is not Haben's will."

Leah snorted, "I remind you, Adamson, I am not a follower of your prophet."

Ben seconded the opinion, "Nor am I."

Nathan nodded "True enough. Do as you will, then." He looked at Leah. "If you wish me to leave, I will."

Leah draw back in mock amazement "What, and have you disobey Neshamah? Unthinkable!"

Nathan's eyes narrowed slightly. "Do not mock what you do not understand, young woman. Do you want me to leave?"

Leah hesitated, unsure. It was true, she knew there was a risk when she harbored any of the Chasidim. No one had ever bothered her before though. There'd never been any real consequences for her actions. But what if this time there was? What did she really owe them, anyhow? Nothing. Not really. Not exactly, anyhow. Still . . . .

Leah frowned, then said, "You can stay. But *you* leave."

She turned abruptly on Ben. "I didn't ask you here, and I don't want you here. Get out."

Nathan said quickly, "If Ben leaves, I leave."

Ben stared darkly at Nathan. "I don't need you to fight my battles."

"I'm not. If you leave, I go, too." Nathan looked at Leah. "Neshamah's message included Ben. I don't understand it, I can't explain it, but I know it's right. If you throw him out, I leave as well."

Anger lit Leah's eyes. "Don't push this, Adamson. I'll let you stay, but not him. If the King Himself stood before me, I wouldn't let him stay."

Nathan looked at Ben and declared quietly, "Then I'll be leaving." He walked to the corner of the room, picked up the pack he'd carried in, and started for the door.

Ben countered sharply, "Don't be a fool, Adamson! You don't have to leave. I'll go."

Nathan did not turn but continued out the door. Ben shrugged slightly then looked at Leah. "It was a pleasure to see you again, Leah. Good luck." He gathered his book and bag, then followed Nathan out the door.

Captives

Athariym paced before the three silent men in his office. Heavy chains bound their hands and feet. Three leaders of the faith, treated as common criminals, waited for Athariym to speak.

Ahab was the oldest in the group. The file on him was extensive. He'd been a leader of the Chasidim for half a century, continually opposing Adam Chata at every turn. But never with violence or malice aforethought. How one so frail could exercise such influence was incredible. The man was well into his seventies, stood just over five feet tall, and looked as though a breath of wind would knock him over. A few strands of white hair lingered on his head. His gnarled hands clutched a cane. Yet, his deep blue eyes showed an inner strength that would surprise those who judged by looks alone. Athariym knew Ahab to be a pillar of faith and strength in the Chasidim.

Chedvah stood beside Ahab. He, too, was elderly, but more hale and taller than Ahab. His hair was just as white, but full and wavy. His hazel eyes displayed the same keen clearness of Ahab's. Chedvah's file was just as exasperating. He had done nothing for which he could be legally detained or publicly humiliated, but he was a thorn in Adam Chata's flesh.

Last of all was Arek. He was the youngest of the three, possibly in his late fifties or early sixties. His file was marked by one attribute alone, perseverance. Nothing had ever rattled Arek. He was a large man, well over six feet tall, with black hair and even blacker eyes. His muscles rippled as he moved. Arek, it was said, was a man who could handle anything. Athariym was about to put Arek to the severest test he could devise.

He hoped. Perhaps if he could maintain a show of authority and menace, his plan would bear more fruit than it had so far. Considering nothing else had gone right, there was little hope that he'd succeed now. But having chosen his course, he'd stick with it. Athariym had expected five leaders to be taken; the guards had found only three. He'd demanded their capture within one hour; it had taken nearly two. It was his plan to cow them into submission, to make them talk by the sheer force of his presence. Not one of them had uttered a single word since he'd had them apprehended. No, the plan was definitely not working.

Athariym glared at his captives. "Don't you realize who I am? And whose authority I wield? I have the power to terminate your miserable lives. Tell me what I want to know! Where is Ben Ramah?"

Ahab looked at his counterparts. Chedvah and Arek nodded slightly to him, appointing him spokesman. Ahab nodded in return, then addressed Athariym. "You wield no power but what was given to you by our King to start with. We, too, are men under authority. Ben Ramah is not of our company, and we have no knowledge of his whereabouts."

Athariym snapped, "You're lying. My contacts have reported Ramah was seen with one of your members earlier today." Athariym picked up the hastily scrawled note he'd been given moments before the Chasidim leaders had been brought in. It stated that Ben Ramah had been spotted near the Bavith, traveling with a known fugitive, Nathan Adamson. The contact had lost sight of them in a crowd of sightseers but was convinced it was Ramah. Of course, Athariym had perhaps fifteen other reports of sightings, as well, but only this one caught his attention. Something about it convinced him it was true.

Athariym waved the paper before the men. "One of your people has him. Where did he take him?"

Again Ahab glanced at the others. Both shrugged; this was news to them. Ahab asked, "Which follower?"

Athariym snorted, "Does it matter? Aren't you all 'of one mind' as you say?

Ahab said, "Unity of purpose does not mean unity of mind. Unlike your superior, we do not claim to read the minds of men. Which follower was seen with Ramah?"

Athariym hesitated, then snapped, "Nathan Adamson. He's wanted for treason. Where is he? You are sheltering him, I know. I want him, now."

Chedvah said calmly, "Nathan went out on his own some days ago. We have not seen him or heard from him since before he left. He is not being sheltered at any of the Chasidim houses that I am aware of."

Athariym mocked, "That you are aware of." He glared angrily. "You wouldn't tell me if you *were* aware of it." He studied the men, then said, "I want Ramah. I want him now. If you don't tell me where he is, you will be executed tomorrow."

Ahab said softly, "One day or ten, it makes no difference. We do not know where he is."

"Then prepare to die."

Chedvah smiled. "We've been prepared for that a long time."

Athariym snarled, "You think this is a joke?"

Chedvah shook his head. "No, I believe you intend to try to carry out your threat."

"Try? What try? I will have you executed, and who can save you?"

Arek replied, "The King we serve is able to deliver us. But if He chooses not to, we would not do other than we are."

Athariym shouted in frustration, "Guard!" The door

swung open and a soldier entered. He saluted smartly. Athariym ordered, "Take these men to the city center. Then announce it throughout all of Tebel-Ayr that they are to be killed if Ben Ramah is not delivered by sunrise. Understand? Take them now."

The guard snapped off another salute. "Yes, sir." He shoved Ahab roughly. The older man stumbled and fell to his knees. Arek caught him. He helped Ahab to his feet, then faced the guard. "There was no need for that," he said quietly. Then with no apparent effort, he twisted the shackles off his own wrists. The guard and Athariym froze in fear.

Arek said, "We will go wherever you tell us. Treat these men with the respect they deserve." The guard looked at Athariym, then took Ahab's arm and guided him toward the door.

Athariym recovered some of his composure and muttered, "I will execute them. I will. And Adam Chata will thank me for it. We should have done this years ago. Wipe out the whole lot of them. That will do it." He looked anxiously at the window, judging the hour. He still had time to save face . . . and his life. It would work. This time, this plan would work. It would. It would . . . wouldn't it?

Ben caught up with Nathan before the man reached the first corner away from Leah's house. He fell in step and said, "You know she's right. It is me Adam Chata wants. I don't know why he would care, but he does." He remembered yesterday's vision of Adam Chata's rage. He tried to ignore it and added, "You don't have to leave on my account."

Nathan repeated, "I'm not."

"Then why?"

Nathan shrugged, unsure of his own motives. "It seemed like the thing to do at the time, I guess."

Ben chuckled, then said cryptically, "I see."

Nathan grinned but kept walking. Ben asked, "Where

are you going to go? Do you have people who can hide you?"

Nathan shook his head. "There are many but none I would endanger like that. You don't put family in that kind of position. What about you?"

Ramah shrugged. "I've got markers I can call in. I'll be safe enough."

Nathan raised an eyebrow in disbelief. "You have friends you trust that much?"

"No, but I know enough to keep them quiet."

"The politics of intelligence." Nathan could not disguise the disgust in his voice. "It's a hollow game, Ben. And an empty promise. Whatever you think you know, someone else also knows, and knows more. You can bet that anyone you have a file on, Adam Chata has one on as well. And probably more complete than yours."

"I'll take that chance. I've done well for myself this long. Don't worry about me."

Nathan stopped and faced the younger man. "I won't. But I do care. I've hated you for the past two years for what you've tried to do to my son, turning him away from me to serve your governor. But now, after last night . . . ." Nathan studied Ben's face, then continued, "I see something else in you, Ramah. It was no accident you came to Leah's. You know it as well as I do. You came in an enemy. I want to believe you leave a friend." Nathan fell silent, considering and praying. He nodded slightly, then said "I'm going to seek sanctuary in the catacombs. If you want me, that's where I'll be, until or unless Neshamah sends me elsewhere. Come with me, if you like, or go your own way. It's up to you."

Ben stared in fascination at the man. "You're most unusual, Adamson. You're telling me where I can find you? What's to prevent me from buying my freedom with your life? You are wanted, you know."

"I know."

"Then why? Why tell me? You don't know me; you don't owe me anything. Why?"

Nathan shrugged. "Like I said, I see something in you."

"What?"

"Maybe I see myself, like I was before. I sold out every-thing . . . and everyone I cared about to keep my power and position for as long as I did. It cost me my wife and may yet cost me my children. But I was wrong, and I know it. You have a chance to avoid all that, to turn away and start over. That's the real gift of Haben, to make us over new in His image. Don't wait fifty years like I did."

Ben listened, then shook his head. "You people. You never stop preaching, do you? Haben Jah is the answer to everything."

Nathan shrugged. "He is. And I am what I am. Will you come with me?"

Ben considered, then shook his head. "No. I can handle this on my own. I don't need a savior."

Nathan stuck out his hand. "Take care of yourself, then. I'll see you again."

Ben hesitated, then accepted Nathan's hand. "You're different, Adamson. But good luck. If I can help you, I will."

Nathan smiled wryly, but said nothing. He shook hands with the younger man, then turned away, crossed the street and disappeared down an alley.

Ben watched him go, then shrugged and turned away. His mind jumped away from the past to the immediate "opportunity" of the present. Where could he go? Should he go anywhere? The prospect of going back to the palace and confronting Adam Chata was not to his liking. Ben felt an unusual reluctance to face his boss. He'd commit-ted no trespass, surely, in trying to learn about the Chasi-dim and Neshamah. That was his primary motivation, af-ter all. He'd sold bigger fables than that before. Why not sell this one?

Ben began walking slowly, without any clear direction

in mind. His thoughts raced ahead to what might be the consequences of his various options. Facing the Governor was too daunting. Perhaps later, but not yet. Ben had a few loose ends to tie up, some facts to assimilate. Later, maybe, when the odds were more in his favor. So, if not the palace, where? Who owed him the biggest debt? A thought struck him cold. Nathan's first thought had been protection of others. Ben's was only for self-preservation. Ben still couldn't get over the strangeness of the man. The fact he was willing to defend Ben for no reason at all, was bizarre.

Well and good, but not helpful now. Where should he go? Ben turned another corner and found himself approaching a listening post. The post was a small, four by eight feet, building designed to shelter one soldier at a time. During his shift, which lasted sunup to sundown, or vice versa, it was his duty to pass messages from the palace along to street criers. The criers were generally young men and women, picked from the Governor's labor rosters. The Governor would send his message to the soldier, who would pass it to the criers, who would announce it in the streets. There were one hundred such posts throughout Tebel-Ayr: thirty in the commerce center and seventy in the housing areas surrounding it. The criers were sworn to carry the messages exactly as received. Death was the penalty for a false word. Criers were to be trusted.

The criers wore distinctive white robes, tight skullcaps, and carried swinging lanterns, symbol of truth and light. The material for the robes was woven only at the palace; any copy or imitation was forbidden.

Ben drew closer but tried to appear focused on the calendar of events posted on a corner lamppost. Eavesdropping on a message relay was strongly discouraged, if not forbidden outright. There was less chance of passersby hearing part of a message and misinterpreting its meaning. If there was one thing Adam Chata would not tolerate, it was being misinterpreted.

Ben's eyes narrowed as he heard the disquieting buzz, murmurs and mutters that signaled something big afoot. Curious, he drew cautiously near the farthest edge of the crowd, searching for faces that would recognize his. Seeing none, he moved closer and listened.

The soldier was finishing his announcement. "That's it, then. Spread it everywhere."

A messenger raised his hand "Are you sure of this? Are you sure there's no mistake? Not even the Governor would dare seize those three."

Another supported the protest. "And have them executed? There has to be something more to it."

The dispatcher shrugged. "Those were the words as they were passed down. I'll give them again. Ahab, Chedvah, and Arek, leaders of the Chasidim cult, have been convicted of treason, resulting from the disappearance of Ben Ramah. Unless he is surrendered in person to Adam Chata by sunrise tomorrow, they will be executed. Every hour thereafter, fifty more members of the Chasidim will be killed until Ramah is released. No more questions. Get the word out." The dispatcher turned and went back into the listening post. Disgruntled and dismayed messengers fanned out along their appointed routes and began shouting, "By the word of Adam Chata, Governor of Tebel-Ayr, high prophet and priest of Golah: Greetings brothers. Be it known that Ahab, Chedvah, and Arek, leaders of the Chasidim . . . ."

Ben groaned silently. This couldn't be happening. They couldn't be executing the leaders. Did Chata know the trouble it would cause? Did he care? Obviously not. Then why?

To get Ramah back. The whole purpose was to trap Ben. But why? Why all this fuss? Ben reasoned it out quickly, but couldn't detect the Governor's hand in all this. Not directly. The insanity was there and plain enough. But not even the Governor would be so blatant. Who, then? Who would be so brash? Someone who didn't know the Chasidim or the delicate balance of power. Someone who wanted to exercise power for power's sake. Someone like himself, ten years ago . . . Athariym. Learning well from his boss, no doubt. Ben ground his teeth in frustration. Now what? He had to stop the executions, that was clear. Ben doubled his pace and began to hurry toward the palace. He couldn't let Athariym destroy all he'd been working for, the elimination of the . . . .

Elimination of the Chasidim. Ben slowed abruptly. Athariym was just doing what Ben had been trying to do for years. Different tactics, maybe, but the same ultimate goal. So why stop him? Stay hidden and let nature take its course. He could, eventually, resurface after Athariym either succeeded in wiping out the Chasidim or failed so miserably Adam Chata would never again question Ramah's plans.

The thought passed as quickly as it came. Ben shook it off angrily. He was a lot of things, but not a murderer. Innocent people would die for a lie, a lie he'd helped create . . . .

So? Let them. Self-preservation, right? Wasn't that the high calling? Why was he so anxious to save any of them? What did he owe any of them?

What did Nathan Adamson owe him? Nothing. But what had he done? Nothing. Not really.

The thought struck Ben *And if the roles were reversed, he'd still do nothing. If he knew where you were, he wouldn't turn you in. Not even to save those men. Would you do the same?*

Ben slowed to a stop. He was near the palace, still on the outskirts of the grounds. The palace was a towering dome on a hill above the city. It could easily house a thousand soldiers, with room to spare. Once a hollow shell, Adam Chata had used his volunteer work force to convert it to offices, living quarters, pantries, all the necessities of life. Ben considered his options carefully. He could walk in easily and announce his "release"; finish off the lie, and no harm would be done. Or he could remain hidden and see how events came down. The second plan was more attractive; less risk to himself. He wouldn't let them go through with the execution, of course, but prudence dictated a wait-and-see attitude.

There was still the problem of where to go. None of the "markers" he'd told Nathan about were particularly appealing at this moment. What Nathan had said about the politics of intelligence was true. What Ben knew, others knew. Or knew other things. And with so many lives at stake, he needed to go to someone he trusted.

Or someone he knew could be trusted. Not the same thing, of course, but maybe more important in the end. The thought of his childhood friend Chalaq returned and would not be dismissed. Chalaq owed Ben nothing but could be trusted to keep his word. Though Ben had not had any contact with him for nearly ten years, now, he still ran across references to him. His old friend was strong in the Chasidim, a leader of impeccable reputation. Many were the times Ben had seen it noted in Chalaq's files where his word had gotten him in trouble, yet he never recanted or backed down. A man that could be trusted. That's what Ben needed now. Ben knew where Chalaq lived: a housing area on the near side of town, not far from the palace. The Chasidim were systematically being gathered into one central location, where they were to be "free" to exercise their beliefs. So went the party line, anyhow. Ben knew—as did the Chasidim—that isolation was one step closer to elimination. But the general populace did not acknowledge the lie. They only saw the beneficent Governor offering a chance for freedom of worship to a recalcitrant and ungrateful people, who opposed him unmercifully. Was it any wonder sympathy for the Chasidim was not widespread? Adam Chata provided everything, and they refused to accept. Maybe they should be eliminated.

Ben was beginning to hate the sound of his own propaganda. And himself for creating it. What kind of person was he, anyhow? Maybe Chalaq would know. One thing for sure, Chalaq would tell him. No question about it.

Ben walked quickly but cautiously toward Chalaq's home. He kept an eye open for anyone that might know him, or recognize him, or otherwise betray him. But the streets were fairly empty. At this hour of the day most people were either working for the Governor, in school, or deeply engrossed in their day's pursuits. Ben slipped unnoticed past the palace, then doubled his pace. It took him just under twenty minutes to reach the home of his former friend. So intent was Ben on getting there, he hadn't once given thought to what he would do when he arrived. He slowed as he approached the Chasidim housing area.

The houses were identical to those throughout all of Tebel-Ayr: sandstone cubicles meant for occupying, not enjoying. But these houses were less well-built, more weatherworn, than the rest of the city. Ben knew that inferior materials had been used in the construction. Governor's orders. And the crews that had worked here were not master craftsmen. No, the good workers were assigned elsewhere. Only the weakest, poorest, least-motivated laborers were directed here.

Ben came to a complete stop beside Chalaq's house. The name of Haben Jah was neatly engraved across the door; hand carved, a true labor of love. Ben wondered, *What do I say?* Why was he even here? Maybe he should leave. Quickly. Now, before he made a total fool of himself.

The battle raged briefly inside, then was still. He should stay. Knock. Tell Chalaq that Neshamah had sent him. Ask to come inside. Tell Chalaq the whole truth, and see what happened from there. But the first step was to knock.

The instructions were crystal-clear, and Ben did not doubt for a moment they were *not* of his own making. But he'd been out of control for days, now . . . no, not out of control. Maybe under control, for the first time. It was a daunting thought. Ben drew himself up, hesitated a moment, then knocked once.

The door opened immediately. Chalaq stood before Ben, smiling, eyes bright with joy. He said solemnly, "Come in, old friend. I've been expecting you."

Pathways

Nathan arrived at the catacombs an hour after he and Ben parted. Four rugged stone pillars marked the corners of what had once been a tomb: the entrance to an abandoned cemetery. Neglected and abused markers lay scattered across the area. The remains of once-tall monuments were shattered and broken. Whether the destruction was natural or deliberate, Nathan didn't know. It didn't really concern him right now, either. His attention focused on the empty tomb at the farthest end of the cemetery. It was once believed to be the tomb of Haben Jah Himself, though mostly through legend and superstition. Now it stood silent and abandoned, quietly waiting for any who might seek sanctuary within. Beneath its walls lay the catacombs.

The catacombs were built long ago. They were a series of tunnels and passageways that crisscrossed beneath the city of Tebel-Ayr. Their original purpose could only be guessed. Some said they were for hiding and escape, as they were used by the Chasidim now. Others believed they were service roads, with easy access from one end of town to another. Still another theory was that they were waterways. Nathan never bothered to study their origins. He was more concerned with their current use. Each Chasidim house had appointed leaders who were taught the layout of the catacombs. To ensure that no one person could betray the entire system, each elder knew only a part of the puzzle. Nathan's house marked their entrance

here, but he knew there were countless others throughout the city. Although he'd never had much occasion to
need them before, he'd been taught the way as a matter of
course.

Nathan made sure there were no watching eyes, either
on the ground or in the air, then slipped quietly across the
field into the tomb. He felt a slight chill as he passed
through the entrance, and a line from the Kathab came to
him: "Why seek ye the living among the dead? He is not
here; He is risen." So said the angels to the women who
came to anoint Haben Jah's body after His death. Risen,
indeed. Haben's death and resurrection had meant life to
countless millions who followed Him. It seemed fitting
that His tomb, still empty, would still provide life for His
followers now. Nathan pushed on the third stone from the
bottom at the far left corner of the back wall. There was a
soft "click," and a portion of the wall turned slightly inward. Nathan pushed inside, then slid the door firmly
shut. Finally he was safe.

No light penetrated the tunnels at this level. Guided by
memory and prayer Nathan followed the course he was
shown, turning left, right, left, right, bypass the next
opening, turn left, bypass two openings, turn right . . . all
the while either angling deeper or climbing higher with
the rise and fall of the slopes. The catacombs were not for
the weak of heart. Unless one maintained the Light inside, the darkness was oppressive. But Haben Jah was the
Light in the darkness, the One True Light come into the
world. To follow Him was to walk in light yourself.
Nathan passed confidently through the outer maze, and
headed for the sanctuary within.

Leah stood before her easel and stared at the blank canvas. She'd been staring at it for nearly an hour, waiting
for inspiration, but none came. There was inside only a
blankness, and an emptiness she couldn't explain. Leah
picked up a brush, dipped it in the water, then stared at

the paint brush. What color? What color was she feeling? Blue? Gray? Black? How do you paint nothing?

The young woman aimlessly chose red and began brushing the canvas with gentle strokes. Red could be flowers, if they still existed. Not in Tebel-Ayr, of course, but somewhere. Or, red could be a sunrise, or a sunset, it was hard to tell which in the haze that shrouded the city. Red could also be anger. Or pain. Or blood. Innocent blood.

Leah laid the brush down carefully, then stared at the canvas. This was ridiculous. All this turmoil over a stranger and a snake. She was glad they were gone. She'd never wanted them there in the first place. Neshamah had been wrong to send them to her. That's whose fault it *really* was—Neshamah's. He should have known there would be trouble . . . .

The strong quiet voice behind her did not startle the woman, "I did know. I presented you with an opportunity to aid my people."

Leah said flatly, "And I turned them away." She turned to face Kadosh Neshamah. She studied the Man carefully, then asked, "Are you telling me Ben Ramah is one of Your children? That he has truly accepted Haben Jah as Lord? Ben Ramah has but one lord, and that's himself."

Neshamah said quietly, "What is that to you? I asked only that you follow Me." He paused, then added, "As you once pledged you would do."

Leah shook her head. "I was just a child. I didn't know what I was doing. You can't hold me to that. No court in this land would accept that commitment as legal and binding.

"In this land, perhaps not. But there is a Higher Court, and One Who judges righteously, not according to human wisdom or logic."

Leah turned away from Neshamah. "I refuse to help Ben Ramah."

Neshamah ignored her declaration and said, "There will be other opportunities set before you to act on or repent of that decision. Ahab, Chedvah, and Arek have been imprisoned by Adam Chata."

Leah spun around. "Arek is in prison? For what?"

"For obeying Me, child."

Leah shook her head angrily and demanded, "What offense? How serious? Arek was my friend. He helped me more than anyone else when . . . ." She broke off, then asked, "What can I do? How can I help?"

Neshamah shrugged. "You had opportunity before and refused it."

"That was different. I don't care what happens to Ben Ramah. But Arek . . . ."

"Arek is being held for aiding Ben Ramah. To help one is to help the other."

Leah stared at Neshamah in disbelief. Her eyes narrowed dangerously as she accused, "You knew that all along, didn't you? What a cheap maneuver."

Neshamah's voice became stern, "I know all ends, Leah Bataqab. No 'maneuver,' as you call it, is cheap. The redemption of every soul came at greater cost than you can ever imagine." Leah's eyes widened slightly in fear. She'd not heard Neshamah speak so forcefully before. She eyed the Man with renewed respect, waiting.

Neshamah noted her expression, then continued. "You will have opportunity to aid Arek. To do so is to aid Ben Ramah. It also will aid Nathan Adamson, yourself, your brother, your family, and ultimately Haben Jah Himself. No act of obedience is performed in a vacuum. Like a pebble thrown in a pond, it creates ripples that flow outward to touch many, many lives. But you must choose what course you will take. Continue in your hatred of Ben Ramah and others will suffer consequences you never foresaw."

Leah turned away and said flatly, "You don't know what he did to me."

"I know what was done *for* you. Have you repaid that debt in full?"

Leah glared angrily, but remained silent. Neshamah continued, "Until you have, you remain a bondservant. The lien on your service remains in effect. Whether you choose to obey is up to you, but the debt remains."

Leah continued to glare angrily at the floor, sullen and bitter. She muttered, "I will not help Ben Ramah." She looked up at Neshamah defiantly. "I won't. I'll do all I can for Arek and the others, but I won't help Ramah."

Neshamah shrugged. "It is your choice. Wrong, but still your choice."

An urgent knocking began on her door, and Daniel's voice called anxiously, "Leah, Leah!"

Leah turned away from Neshamah and went to the door. She opened it slowly. Daniel's face was dark with anger and concern. He stepped inside and said, "Are you OK? They weren't here, were they?"

"Who? What are you talking about?" Leah hadn't often seen Daniel so upset.

"The Tabbach soldiers. They're making a house-to-house search. Your 'company' may be in danger."

Leah shook her head. "My 'company' is gone."

Daniel relaxed slightly. "Good." He studied his sister a moment, then asked, "What's going on, Leah? Are you involved in this?"

"In what?" Leah avoided her brother's eyes.

"The arrest of the Chasidim and Ben Ramah's disappearance. There's even talk on the street that Adam Chata is trying to capture Neshamah Himself."

Leah looked up in disgust. "What? You're not serious. Only a total fool would believe that Neshamah could be captured."

Daniel said softly "Who do you think this world consists of? There are only two kinds of people, Leah, fools and the Chosen. Some are fools because they don't know; others because they do and choose not to act on it."

Leah growled, "Don't preach to me this morning. I've had enough preaching for one day."

Daniel studied his sister again, then said finally, "I'm going to see Uncle Nadiyb. Maybe he can do something to help Arek. He does hold considerable influence in the palace."

Leah gasped in mock surprise. "You would ask Uncle for a favor? Why, Daniel, I would never have dreamed it of you."

Daniel glared at Leah coldly. His voice was stern as he said quietly, "I owe the man, Leah. I'll do anything and everything I can to win his release." Without another word Daniel turned and walked out.

Leah started to say, "Daniel, wait . . . ." but stopped. Let him go. She'd come up with her own plan. Her brother would understand, later. But now, to business. How could she free Arek? Neshamah said he'd been arrested for helping Ramah. And Adam Chata wanted Ben Ramah back. The answer was simple. Send Ramah back. Or take him back. Or have him taken . . . . Leah considered the options, then nodded to herself. It made sense to her. Perfect sense. And so easy, too. If she could find him again. But, then, maybe she wouldn't have to. Neshamah had said she'd have opportunity to help Ramah again. She'd help him, all right. She'd help everybody. She whispered to no one in particular "Send him back here. I'll help him. I really will." Silently she made her plans.

Ben sat across from Chalaq and studied his old friend closely. The years since they had parted had been hard for Chalaq, he decided. Though the man spoke with joy of his marriage, his three children, and his work as a copyist, Ben sensed that not all had been easy. The deep lines in his face, the sprinkling of gray in his once-black hair, the slightest of hesitations as he talked, all were clues to Ben that life was difficult. Of course, being one of the Chasidim, you would expect that. The house furnishings, too, spoke of hardship. All the furniture—what there was of it—was worn, patched, repatched, and repaired. Ben knew from the layout of the rooms that this was a two-bedroom house, yet Chalaq spoke of three children. Tight quarters, no doubt. Yet there was no bitterness in the man's voice, only a calm presentation of the facts.

As Chalaq finished describing his latest job, recopying two volumes of the history of Tebel-Ayr, he said wryly, "But you didn't come here to check on an old friend."

Ben shrugged. "Not exactly." He eyed Chalaq and asked, "What did you mean you'd been expecting me? How? Why?"

Chalaq considered his answer carefully, then said, "Let's say I've often thought about you, and hoped I would get the chance to talk to you again."

Ben shook his head. "There's more to it than just hopes and thoughts. I know that, now." Ben hesitated, then plunged in. "I'm here because of Kadosh Neshamah. I needed to find out about Him, and I thought you could tell me."

Chalaq looked slightly surprised. "You needed to know about Neshamah? Why?"

"I do, that's all." Somehow, telling Chalaq he had been ordered to capture Kadosh Neshamah was too absurd to mention.

"And my name just popped into your head."

Ben admitted, "Something like that. Something very close to that, in fact."

Chalaq suppressed a smile, unsuccessfully. Ben noted it, grimaced, but waited for Chalaq to respond. Chalaq said softly, "Well, Ben, you 'popped' into my head today, too. You're right. There is more to it than thoughts and hopes. I've never stopped praying for you all these years. The Kathab teaches us we are to pray for the leaders of our country so we might live in peace. So I've been praying for you that way. But I've also prayed for you as my friend, that you would one day open your heart to our

Lord Haben Jah. I was praying for you this morning, in fact, when I had the thought that you would come today, asking about Him."

Ben took this silently. Somehow, after talking with Nathan, it didn't surprise him. It puzzled him, confused him, even scared him, but it didn't surprise him.

Chalaq continued, "I mostly ignored it as wishful thinking. But it wouldn't go away. Finally I sent Judith and the children to her mother's for the day." He smiled. "A good thing, too. Discussing anything is a real chore with a five-, a three-, and a one-year-old running around. I spent the morning just reading and praying, not knowing what to expect, if anything. And now here you are."

Ben asked, "But you didn't know? When you first had your 'thought,' didn't you know it was Neshamah telling you I would come?"

Chalaq studied Ben. The question obviously surprised the man. He asked, "What do you know about Neshamah?"

Ben was torn between, "Not enough," and "Too much." In the end he said only, "Very little."

Chalaq prompted, "Like . . . ."

Ben thought rapidly over the past hours, then said, "Well, I do know He exists. That's a major concession."

"But Heylel, the King's enemy knows He exists, too. And trembles at His name."

"Until yesterday I wouldn't have admitted the King exists. Not the way you Chasidim say He does. We believe the King is a superstition, a name given to explain forces that couldn't otherwise be explained. The truth of the King is power: power in nature, power in each individual. But you talk of the King as a person."

"You said, 'We believe.' We who? I know that's what the Governor teaches, but do you believe it?"

"I did."

"Past tense. Do you now?"

Ben looked Chalaq straight in the eyes and admitted, "I

don't know. I don't think so. Not after actually seeing Kadosh Neshamah." He paused, clinging to his old defenses, and added, "But that doesn't prove Neshamah is the King. And it doesn't make me a follower of Haben Jah, either."

"No, it doesn't," Chalaq agreed. "But it does open the door to questions. It's a place to start."

Ben considered this, then nodded. "It's a place to start."

Chalaq smiled broadly.

Daniel marched angrily from Leah's house. His sister's callousness might be contrived, but it still had the power to irritate him. He forced himself to slow down, however. "The wrath of man works not the righteousness of God." The time to deal with Leah would come, but not now. Now was a time for cool heads and all the wisdom Haben Jah could give him.

Daniel walked quickly to his home and scribbled a note for Ruth. She was out visiting with the twins, he knew. Not that she would expect him home. Daniel should be hard at work at the quarry, cutting stones for the Bavith. His father had been a stonecutter; now Daniel followed in his steps. In more ways than one, he hoped.

Daniel shed his work clothes and quickly changed into a clean shirt and pants. He tossed his heavy leather coveralls to one side of the room, then wondered if he would ever need them again. When he'd heard that Arek and the others had been arrested, he'd left his work crew immediately. He'd have some explaining to do when he came back. If he was allowed to come back.

Daniel headed out the door, then stopped. Just where was he going, anyhow? His first intention was to petition Uncle Nadiyb. But while it was true Nadiyb had Adam Chata's ear, it was equally true his uncle had no love for the Chasidim. He wouldn't intervene for Arek without a good reason.

Daniel paused, his hand on the doorknob. There was a

very good reason for Nadiyb to do all that Daniel would ever ask, but the young man wasn't ready to force that issue, yet. What he knew, he would not reveal until the proper time. This wasn't it. There were other channels. Arek had friends in Tebel-Ayr. Although like all the Chasidim he held no position of authority, he was still respected throughout the city. If Daniel could muster enough popular support, maybe he could dissuade Adam Chata from carrying out this insane plan. Daniel nodded to himself. He'd start with the Chasidim, then go from there. He'd make it work, for Arek's sake.

As he walked quickly towards the north end of the city, Daniel reflected on what he owed Arek and all the Chasidim. After his parents disappeared, Nadiyb took over as guardian. It was convenient that no bodies were ever found, nor his parents officially declared dead. Had they been, a will would have been read. And Daniel knew that his father had appointed Arek to raise his children, something Nadiyb would never tolerate, or admit.

Nadiyb forbade Arek to see Daniel or Leah. But the Chasidim leader had found ways to communicate with them through the years. He'd sent letters, always through surreptitious means. Sometimes Daniel found them at school, sometimes at home, sometimes on the street. The letters spoke warmly of his father and mother, of their faith, their love for Haben Jah, their hopes and dreams for their children. The letters became Daniel's link to his parents. Arek told of the search that continued to find them; never shielding Daniel from the truth, but constantly exhorting him to grow in the faith. Arek always included large passages from the Kathab, continuing the education Daniel's father had begun with his son. Daniel had studied the verses, and had written back, leaving his letters in the same mysterious drop places he'd found Arek's. It was a correspondence that had blossomed into a deep love for Arek and for all the man stood for. Daniel knew Arek had written to Leah, too. And early on, she had responded in kind. But growing up in the house of Nadiyb Bataqab had been harder on Leah than Daniel, primarily because she was so like her uncle in temperament and will, though Daniel would never tell her so. Yet he had watched as his sister increasingly reflected the cynical, manipulative attitudes of their guardian. Daniel wasn't at all sure he liked the woman she was becoming. Still, she belonged to Haben Jah. He would guide her in the end. "None that You have given Me have I lost," Haben had prayed to His Father. It was true then, true now, true forever.

Daniel's thoughts occupied him in his trek across the city, until he reached the door he was seeking. Arek's son lived close to the palace; it would be as good a place to start as any. Daniel hesitated, then knocked loudly.

There was a sound of shuffling and scurrying, then the door opened a crack. Daniel couldn't see inside, but a timid voice whispered, "Go away. Leave us alone."

Daniel was taken aback. He demanded, "I have to speak to Bagad. It's about Arek."

"Bagad isn't here."

"Where is he?"

"Gone. He's not here. I'm not here, either. You haven't seen me, nor heard me. As you love Arek, go away from here, quickly. Before more trouble falls."

The door slid shut. Daniel heard the bolt being thrown, then silence. He shook his head. It would be useless to pursue anything further here. However strong Arek was in the faith, his son did not share his father's convictions. Let them be. There were others who could help. Daniel would just have to find them. Determined, he set out again.

Betrayal

Leah watched impatiently out her window. Time. Time. Time was passing, and things weren't happening right. The woman looked over at Sharath Shinan and asked, "Did he get the message? Why isn't he here?"

The cat calmly licked his front paw and carefully groomed his ears. He looked disdainfully at Leah and purred, "He got the message. I gave it to him myself. He'll be coming soon. Mirmah does not respond well to being summoned."

Leah shrugged, "He'll get over it. And he'll be truly appreciative of this one. Mirmah will love nothing more than to bring down one of Adam Chata's own."

Sharath drawled slowly, "As you will."

Leah glared at the cat, "I'm doing this for Arek."

"Sure you are." The cat stretched indolently. "Having exhausted all other avenues for securing his release, you resort to betrayal as a last hope." The cat spat. "I have heard it before, or excuses equally feeble. So spoke Ben Shinown, before betraying Haben Jah."

Leah turned away from the cat and said flatly, "Ben Shinown betrayed innocent blood. Ben Ramah has never been innocent in his life." She looked out the door and said, "Here he comes." Mirmah's height and girth were hard to miss; well over six feet tall, and close to 275 pounds. His unkempt black hair hung loosely at his shoulders. He wore leather breeches and heavy boots.

Sharath spat again and walked from the room. Leah was aware of his leaving but ignored it. She'd make that right, too, later. She watched Mirmah stroll along the path, in no apparent hurry. Leah growled slightly but swallowed her ire. She needed Mirmah. She pasted on her most pleasant smile and waited patiently for the man to enter.

Mirmah had been a classmate of hers. He had been enamored of her, though Leah detested him. When Leah had rebuffed his advances in favor of Ben Ramah, Mirmah had appealed to her uncle for her hand. Nadiyb saw no advantage in the union and had refused him. Leah thought silently, *I guess I do owe you that one, uncle.* Rather than risk creating a formidable enemy, Leah had arranged for Mirmah to meet Deborah, her cousin. The match worked, and Mirmah and Deborah were living happily ever after, or so it was told. But Mirmah had held a grudge against Ben Ramah. This plan of Leah's could settle that debt, as well.

Mirmah sauntered up and entered without knocking. He surveyed Leah's paintings, then drawled, "I was told you wanted to see me. Something about a mutual friend in need. What do you want?"

Leah smiled. "Direct and to the point. Good to see you, too, Mirmah."

Mirmah shrugged. "I left my post to come here. What is this about?"

"How would you like to be in on the capture of Ben Ramah?"

Mirmah's eyes glittered, then narrowed. "How?"

"You have a message post. You can pass word on the street. I know Ramah is running, and I suspect looking for a safe place to hide. I'd like for him to know he can come here."

"So you can hide him?" Mirmah laughed harshly. "How does that benefit me?"

Leah shook her head. "You miss the point. I want Ramah to come here so you can turn him in."

Mirmah studied Leah closely. "Why should he trust you?"

Leah shrugged. "Let's say I have reason to believe he will, no questions asked. Trust me, he'll take the offer."

"And why not turn him in yourself?" That's more your style, isn't it?"

"I intend to be with you when you turn him in. I need him to bargain for . . . for a friend."

"What friend?"

Leah shook her head. "An old friend. It doesn't matter."

"It does to me. What friend?"

Leah frowned, then admitted, "Arek, one of the Chasidim leaders."

Mirmah nodded. "I know who he is. What's he to you?"

Leah hesitated a moment. "It was after my parents . . . disappeared. Arek tried to help Daniel and me find out what happened. He wouldn't let me give up." Leah said slowly, "There were times he was the only one I could talk to that understood. I feel like I owe him for that. I'd like to help him."

Mirmah's voice was laced with skepticism. "Of course. How altruistic."

Leah glared at Mirmah. "That doesn't concern you, Mirmah. Do you want in on Ramah's capture or not?"

Mirmah considered the proposition, then nodded. "I guess. Why not? It might be interesting to watch the man squirm." He nodded again, "I'll help. What do you want me to do?"

"Pass the word quietly. Then be ready to come when I call." Leah had worked out all the details prior to Mirmah's arrival. "Deborah hasn't been to see me in ages. If she could come for a visit, I could send her to you when Ramah arrives. Then all you have to do is come get him."

Mirmah thought it over, then agreed. "It sounds good. I'll do it." He looked at the relief in Leah's eyes and smiled. "You do hate him as much as I do, don't you?"

Leah nodded slowly, "Maybe more."

"Then let's trap a snake." Mirmah laughed and sauntered back out the door.

Leah walked to her easel and absently stared at the red streaks she'd begun earlier. Red. Red like pain. Like anger. Like hatred. Red. She'd seen red, then, too. Screaming, raging, vengeful wrath . . . .

"I hate you! I hate you!" Leah screamed violently at her professor. "How could you use me like that? I trusted you! I even loved you! You filthy . . . ." Rage choked the words in her throat as she remembered the scene. They were standing outside her uncle's house.

Ben shrugged nonchalantly. "Fortunes of war, Leah. You got what you wanted, and so did I."

Leah was aghast. "What I wanted? I didn't want anything from you. I gave you everything, and you used me!"

Ben arched an eyebrow. His voice was cool as he said, "You wanted to hurt your uncle. You told me that more than once. Dating me was just another means to that end. Or did you forget?"

Leah screamed, "I never said that! You used me to get Uncle Nadiyb's endorsement for your appointment!"

"Which you worked so diligently to secure for me. And I do appreciate it. But your motives weren't exactly pure either, were they?"

"My motives? I had no motives. I loved you."

Ramah laughed harshly. "Your only love is tormenting your uncle. But he didn't fall for it this time, did he? You never expected him to approve of you and me together. And when he did . . . ." Ben chuckled. "You outsmarted yourself, Leah Bataqab. You're just fortunate I didn't follow up his advice and marry you."

Leah's eyes grew wide with horror and revulsion. "Marry you?" Marry you? "

Ben shrugged. "Don't worry, my dear. I have no intention of humoring your uncle to that extent. Now, if you'll

excuse me, I have a class to teach." Ben smiled, then
walked away, whistling.

Leah stared after him, then screamed again. "I hate
you! I hate you!"

At her easel Leah whispered again. "More. Much
more."

It took Nathan nearly two hours to reach the sanctuary. The sanctuary was little more than a room off the
main passageway. As no one knew the true purpose of the
catacombs, so no one knew the original purpose of the
various chambers. But it now served well as a storehouse.
Here Nathan would find lanterns, oil, and a carefully
tended flame that never went out. The Chasidim kept the
sanctuary stocked with food, water, blankets, and, most
precious of all, copies of the Kathab. The sanctuary was
not meant for prolonged hiding but was a temporary
place of refuge in times of greatest peril. Nathan stepped
into the dimly lit chamber, then drew back immediately.

Someone was already present. Nathan listened intently. Several someones were there, from the sound of the
conversations. Low voices talked softly, men, women, and
an occasional child's laughter, quickly shushed. There
must be quite a crowd. Nathan felt a strange reluctance
to have his presence known. He risked a quick look inside,
careful not to be seen.

Twenty or thirty bodies filled the small chamber. They
were seated around the small fire, probably in family
groups. Children huddled with adults, held close and
quiet. It was cramped; no one moved around. You
couldn't, without walking on someone else. Nathan
thought he recognized some of the faces as members of his
own Chasidim house, but he couldn't be sure. What were
they doing here? Was this because of him? How could it
be? After all, it wasn't that uncommon for one of the Chasidim to rebel against the Governor. But it never brought

trouble to the others. Not directly. Not immediately, anyhow.

Nathan strained to hear some of the conversation, hoping it would give him some clue as to who, what, and why this crowd was. Yet no one seemed inclined to discuss anything of importance. Nathan debated what to do next. If he was the cause of trouble, revealing his presence could further harm his brothers and sisters in Haben Jah. Yet this might be totally unconnected to himself. The only way to find out was . . . .

Nathan stepped forward into the light and stood still, letting the others become aware of him. A few heads turned; most ignored him. One man nodded to him. Another said, "This room can hold no more. You will have to find other shelter."

Nathan asked, "What brings you here? What has happened?"

More heads turned, and sharply. Someone let out a low whistle. "Don't you know? Why are you here, if you don't?"

Nathan countered, "The sanctuary has always been open to anyone. I was seeking a place of retreat for a few hours until I received instructions. Why are you here?" Nathan couldn't identify a lead spokesman, so spoke to the crowd in general.

There were low mutters, then from the back of the room a man's voice complained bitterly, "It's a purge, I tell you. Adam Chata has finally had enough, and is going to destroy us all."

Nathan was incredulous. "A purge? Be reasonable, brother. Adam Chata knows better than that."

The speaker muttered angrily, "Tell that to Ahab. Or Arek, or Chedvah. The Governor has arrested them."

"They have been arrested before."

Another voice from the opposite side of the room said, "But never threatened with execution."

Nathan's confusion grew. "Execution? For what?"

"Does the Governor need a reason?"

Nathan's frustration mounted as voices answered him from all sides. He demanded, "Is there one elder here who can give me clear answers?"

No one spoke. Nathan eyed the group carefully. He could not disguise the reproach in his voice. "I see. Either none present, or none willing to step forward and be recognized."

A soft chuckle came from the near wall. Nathan turned to see an older man, perhaps sixty, heavyset, bald, dressed in work clothes, stand up. He said, "I cannot step forward without stepping on toes." He let the double meaning fall on all that had ears to hear, then continued, "But I am an elder. We are of the Chen house. I am Amats. Since you know this place I wager you are of our house, though your face is unfamiliar to me."

Nathan nodded. "As is yours to me. I am still fairly new to the house. I am Nathan Adamson."

A disgruntled murmur tore through the crowd. Nathan saw several eyes quickly averted, others closed. No, they hadn't seen him. Couldn't recognize or identify him. Didn't know him.

Amats said, "Then you do know why we are here."

"No, I don't. I am wanted, I admit. I took my children to Yada, and the Governor wants me because of it. I returned to Tebel-Ayr because Haben Jah would have me be a witness for Him in the Governor's palace. When, how, or where has not been shown me, as yet. I came to the sanctuary to wait for instructions. Again I ask, why are you here?"

"Ben Ramah, the Governor's aide, is missing. Adam Chata believes you are tied in with his disappearance. The Governor is holding Ahab and the others, and promises to execute them if Ramah is not found by sunrise."

Nathan's face must have revealed more than he intended, for Amats said, "You know of Ramah?"

Nathan hesitated, then admitted, "I have seen him. But he left the Governor of his own accord."

The man who had insisted on the purge asked sharply, "Do you know where he is?"

"Not now." Nathan was glad he could honestly say it. "We parted before I came here."

Amats asked, "What does he want?"

Nathan shrugged. "I'm not sure he is sure." Adamson's eyes narrowed slightly. "But that still does not explain why you are all here in hiding. Why aren't you working to free our leaders?"

Amats looked around on the crowd. None would meet his eye directly. He smiled grimly at Nathan. "You know how it is, brother. Priorities."

Nathan addressed the crowd. "And you think hiding will keep you safe? What do you plan on doing? Hope Adam Chata cools off or forgets you? How long can you hide?"

An unidentified voice muttered, "As long as it takes."

"And how will you know when that is? You don't light a candle, then hide it under a basket! You are light and salt. There is work to be done. Let's go do it."

Nathan eyed the group expectantly, but no one moved. He waited, then said, "I see. I understand all too well." He started to speak again but stopped as a verse from the Kathab whispered in his conscience, *"Who are you to judge another Man's servant? To his own Master he stands or falls."* Nathan swallowed his rebuke, then said simply, "The King be with you, my brothers."

Nathan turned and walked out, back into the darkness. No, not into the darkness. Away from the darkness, into the light. There was work to be done. He prayed silently as he walked, "Lead me, Lord Haben Jah. Show me where to go and what to do now."

A plan began to form in his head. Nathan's eyes widened slightly in fear as he saw it is unfolding before him. He stopped cold, then said softly, "As You will, Lord. As

You will." Nathan hurried back through the silent
catacombs.

"I don't understand these people! Why won't they help?
What's wrong with them, anyhow?" Daniel gave full vent
to his frustration. He was sitting in the home of Shalom,
oldest member of the Chasidim. Shalom was Daniel's last
hope. His entire afternoon had been filled with rejections,
denials, polite rebukes, but no promise of assistance.
Daniel threw up his hands. "Don't they understand
what's going to happen? Adam Chata is going to execute
every last member of the Chasidim if he can. We've got to
do something!"

Shalom poured Daniel a cup of tea. The ancient woman
waited patiently until Daniel's verbal torrent subsided,
then said softly. "I will not excuse all, Daniel. But I do
understand."

"Then help me understand." Daniel's voice was rife
with bitterness. "Arek, Ahab, Chedvah . . . with them
gone, who will lead the Chasidim?"

Shalom said primly, "The same One Who leads us now,
young one. Do you truly believe Haben Jah will be helpless to save if these three perish?"

"No, but, . . ."

Shalom did not let him finish. "No, but, indeed. Search
the Kathab, young one. Your education is obviously in-
complete." A palsied hand pointed across the room to the
lone table. "Bring me the Word, and I will show you."

Daniel rose obediently from the couch beside the old
woman , and retrieved the Kathab from its place of honor,
in full display. The thick layer of dust on the table was
evidence that Shalom was increasingly feeling her age.
She must be well into her nineties by now. Short, plump,
thin silver hair, hard of hearing, slow moving . . . she
walked with two canes, when she walked at all. But her
mind was still sharp, a merciful gift from the Lord Haben
Jah. Daniel knew some of her history. She was a mother

of six, grandmother of eighteen, great-grandmother of who knew how many now. She'd been widowed fifteen years before, after sixty-three years of marriage to the same man. Shalom was a peacemaker, and the Lord's special blessings rested fully on her. She had devoted her life to serving her Lord, her family, and those around her. Even in these declining years, her door was still open to all who would seek her wisdom.

Daniel carried the Kathab back to the couch and handed it to Shalom. She waved it off, saying, "My eyes are too dim to see the words, but they are written in my heart. Go to the first book of the kings of the 'Ibriy, chapter nineteen. Read verses eight through eighteen."

Daniel read silently, then waited. Shalom's eyes were closed; her lips moved slightly as she, too, "read" the verses. When she was done, she opened her eyes and looked at the young man. "What did the prophet say?"

Daniel studied the verses again, then said, "He said that he was the only one left who served the True King, and his enemies were trying to kill him."

Shalom nodded. "And what did the King tell him? Verse eighteen, to make it easy. Read it."

Daniel read, " 'Yet have I left Me seven thousand....' "

"Seven thousand, when the prophet thought he was alone. There is always a remnant, Daniel Bataqab. There will always be a remnant. In the last days, after Haben Jah has returned to carry away His people, the Kathab teaches there will be uncounted multitudes who turn to Him in faith, because of the preaching of a faithful remnant. Do not fear, young one. The hands of the King are never bound by our frailties and limitations. Adam Chata may rule for a season, but a remnant will always remain."

Daniel took in the woman's words silently, trying to let her wisdom sink into his heart. After a moment he said quietly, "Thank you, Shalom."

Shalom smiled crookedly. "Thank the King. It is His

promise, not mine. His Word is much more reliable than my own."

Daniel chuckled slightly. "Amen." Then his face grew troubled and he asked, "Then what do I do about Arek and the others? Nothing? Do I just leave them to die?"

Shalom's eyes twinkled. "They would all three benefit from it, no doubt. They know Who waits for them." She sighed longingly and said, "I know the conflict of the new covenant writer. He told his friends, 'I am in a strait between two, having a desire to depart and to be with Haben Jah, which is far better. Nevertheless, to abide in the flesh is more needful for you.' Haben Jah still wants me here, so here I'll stay. If He is ready to take Arek, Ahab and Chedvah, He will. Otherwise, not even Adam Chata has power to take their lives."

"Then I am to do nothing?"

"Have you prayed, young one?"

Daniel nodded. "I've been praying all day that Haben would help me find a way to save them."

Shalom said sharply, "That's not prayer, young one. That's begging for your will. Proper prayer is asking for His will to be done, and then doing it. Have you asked our Lord what He wants?"

Daniel dropped his eyes at the rebuke, then shook his head. Shalom reached out and placed a gnarled hand on his arm. "Then I suggest you have done nothing for them, yet. Until you have prayed and received His answer, you are wasting your time and theirs. We live to serve Haben Jah. We die to serve Haben Jah. In Him we live and move and have our being. Do you want His help? Seek His will."

Daniel nodded. "I do, Shalom. I do want to see His will done."

Shalom smiled. "Then let us find out what that will is together." She closed her eyes and began to pray silently.

Daniel signed, feeling the burden of his fears lifted. He watched the old woman a moment, then smiled, and followed her example.

Ben unsuccessfully tried to stifle another yawn. Great weariness was on him; partly from lack of sleep, partly from frustration. He was glad Chalaq had stepped out of the room to refill his cup with—Ben shuddered slightly—warm cider. Thankfully, not coffee. Anything but coffee! What manner of man was Nathan Adamson that he could tolerate that vile liquid? No normal person would.

But, then, Nathan wasn't a normal person. Neither was Chalaq, Ben was rediscovering. They had been talking for three hours now, catching up on each other's lives, discussing their families, and, when Ben could avoid it no longer, talking of Haben Jah, Neshamah, and the King. It surprised Ben to find that Chalaq had followed his rise to power closely. He knew when Ben had received his appointments to various committees, what laws and sanctions Ben had created or enacted, even how Ben had replaced certain of his adversaries with confederates more to his liking. It puzzled Ben that Chalaq would know so much about him. More puzzling was why he would want to know. Chalaq credited it to old friendships; Ben remained suspicious.

Of their families, there was little to tell. Ben's parents were living comfortably within the senior settlement provided by the Governor for those of proven faithful service. Ben's father occasionally taught for the Governor, continuing to create new truths as he found them. Ben hadn't seen or spoken to either of his parents in nearly a year. He did receive regular reports on their health and well-being, as befitted a dutiful son and only heir. It was all that was required.

Chalaq, on the other hand, was close to his family, a trait shared by many of the Chasidim. It was a strength the Faithful had maintained in spite of Ben's efforts to the contrary. Try as the government might, they had never completely broken the family unit within the Chasidim. Weakened it, certainly, but never broken it. Haben

Jah's teachings on respect and obedience not only to Himself but to parents and family were too strongly ingrained to be destroyed. The youngest of four children, Chalaq visited his parents frequently. Though he did not specifically say so, Ben got the impression Chalaq was supplying them with food and other provisions. From the looks of Chalaq's house, he had little enough to spare. But what he had he evidently shared.

Ben stifled another yawn. What he wouldn't give for a bed, a blanket, and about twenty-four uninterrupted hours. He shook himself. Not yet. There was too much at stake. Too many lives could hang in the balance . . . . All because of him.

Ben fingered the Kathab as it lay on the table. Chalaq's copy of the book lay beside it, tattered, creased, worn, obviously well-read. Ben's remained pristine. For all the challenges around him, he still hadn't begun to read it. After talking with Nathan, and now Chalaq, he was more afraid than ever to start. Who knew what he would find if he looked inside?

"Yourself, for one thing."

Ben looked up to see Kadosh Neshamah standing before him. Somehow he wasn't surprised. He studied the Man, then asked slowly, "You mean I'm in there? How could I be? I wasn't even born when this was written."

"You are there."

"Why?" Ben's frustration began to boil over. "Why am I in there? Why are You here? Why am I here? What is it You want with me?"

Neshamah said evenly, "You were born for a purpose, Ben Ramah. Your birth was no accident; your life no whim. All that you are, and all that you can and will be is by design. The Kathab will show you who you truly are, and what it is you have been called to do."

Ben stood up angrily. "I am my own master, Kadosh Neshamah. I choose my life and destiny. No one chooses it for me."

"So you might believe. And so it is, to a point. But half-truth is still half-lie. The whole Truth remains before you." Neshamah pointed to the Kathab. "You have heard others talk of Him. You begin to know a little about Him. The time has come to meet Him yourself."

"Meet Who?"

"The Truth. Meet Him, then decide who is master of your life. You do have that choice. But only now."

Chalaq reentered the room carrying a small tray with two cups. He saw Ben standing, and the angry look on his face. Chalaq asked, "What's wrong?"

Ben shook his head angrily. "All of this. Everything! You people, your book, your crazy leader, . . . all of it's wrong. Nothing has been right since I left the palace."

Chalaq set the tray down carefully. "Has something happened since I left?"

Ben's voice was heavy with disgust. "Of course not. What could happen? There's just you and me here, right?"

Chalaq eyed Ben closely. Ben caught the look and said roughly, "I'm not a lunatic. We're not alone here, and you know it." Ben pointed to where Kadosh Neshamah stood silently watching the proceedings, His eyes twinkling in what Ben took as amusement. "He's here, too."

Chalaq looked where Ben was pointing. "Who is here?"

"Neshamah, you fool! Who else?? Am I the only one who sees Him?" Ben was beside himself. "You claim to know Him, but you can't see Him! Why? Why?"

Chalaq said soothingly, "Calm down, Ben, and I'll try to explain."

Ben shouted, "I am calm! I've had it with all of you! You're trying to drive me crazy, aren't you? Is that it? You think you can drive me out of office by making me into a raving lunatic!"

Chalaq said carefully, "That's ridiculous, Ben, and you know it. I didn't invite you here."

"No, but you've been waiting for me. You said so your-self." Irrational anger boiled through Ben. The rage he'd seen so often in the Governor threatened to engulf him. It would, easily, if he'd let it. But a very tiny voice, some-where very deep inside urged caution and restraint. Ben continued to glower and breathed heavily. But he said no more until he felt a semblance of calm returning. He reached over, picked up his Kathab, and firmly stuffed it in his satchel. He said brusquely, "I've taken too much of your time. I'm leaving."

Chalaq shook his head sadly. "Ben, don't go off like this. You don't know what you are doing."

"Yes I do," Ben lied. "I'm going back to where I knew what was going on, back to where this all started. Maybe there I can find some answers that make sense."

Neshamah spoke softly, "Adam Chata has no answers for you, Ben Ramah. Nor any love for you. Your life will be forfeited if you return to the palace. It is appointed unto man once to die, and then comes the judgment. You are not ready for that judgment, yet."

"I'll decide that." Ben ignored the confused look on Chalaq's face, turned and walked away. He knew where he wanted to go now, and directed his steps back to the palace. There was a listening post just outside the gates, where Ben could monitor the comings and goings inside the palace. It had been a favorite hiding place of his as a child, and one of the reasons for his swift rise to power. Ben had always been a good listener. Time to listen again.

When Ben reached the post, he checked quickly to make sure no one was around. Then he squeezed himself between the back wall and the stone fence. Quarters had grown smaller in fifteen years. It would be uncomfort-able, but worth it. At least he'd be out of sight. He settled down to wait and listen. The only sounds were the dron-ing of the city itself: a low murmur of voices, of merchants transacting commerce, wagons, carts, . . . Ben closed his eyes to let the sounds wash over him. Easier to pick out important sounds that way. Fewer distractions . . . .

A shout of triumph woke him suddenly. Ben jumped with a start, coming back to full awareness. How long had passed, there was no way of knowing. It was probably early evening. The corner street lamps were just beginning to glow. Ben thought he could faintly make out the trumpet call summoning the people to worship. He shook his head, trying to clear his thinking, and listened as an excited palace runner repeated his message. "They caught him. They really did it this time. He came out of hiding; probably to save those other three. But we have him now."

The dispatcher conveniently asked the question Ben strained to make out: "Who? Who do we have?"

"Kadosh Neshamah! He's under arrest at the prison. We've got Him! We've finally got Him. The guards are bringing Him to the palace right now."

Ben scrambled uncomfortably from his perch. He could just make out the shouts from the city proper. There must be a procession coming. Ben peered over the fence and tried to make out the figures, but the line was still too far away. He heard the runner continue, "They say they've found Ben Ramah, too, and that he'd gone over to the enemy. He's being held at the prison until the governor decides his fate." Ben's eyes widened in surprise, then he understood. Athariym again. Tying up loose ends. Or trying to. All he was doing was creating greater knots to entangle himself. This whole scheme would come apart when Neshamah disappeared, if they even had him. Ben would deal with his apprentice later.

The procession from the city drew closer. Ben could make out faces finally. Athariym led the procession as Ben figured. Get in the limelight as much as possible. That's how to rise in power. Ben knew it well. Behind Athariym were the elite soldiers, called into service for this auspicious occasion. The common Tabbach soldier was clothed in black and gray. The palace guard wore the silver and black, signifying advanced training and rank. Only the Governor's elite forces wore the shimmering white robes of wrath. It indicated to all who saw them the terrifying severity of the occasion. No common prisoner, here, if the elite guard were escorting him. A full regiment of thirty guards surrounded the victim. Nice touch. Athariym had planned this well. Ben grimaced. All the more reason to bring him down hard.

Between the cadre of guards Ben could make out a lone figure, walking shackled and bound. His head was bare, his face marred from a beating. It took Ben several moments to identify the features, so badly swollen was the face. But recognition sank in finally, and Ben's breath left him with a sharp whistle. Nathan Adamson marched grimly between the guards, his head unbowed.

Ben watched, stricken, as the procession passed by. He could still hear the runner giving details of the capture, but it held little meaning to him. Ben's stomach twisted into a tight knot. He whispered hollowly, "I didn't tell anyone. I swear I didn't. I didn't tell." Would Nathan know? Somehow, Ben had to tell him. Whatever had happened, he hadn't been part of it. And it was important that Nathan knew.

The procession passed just under Ben's perch, turned left at the gate, and marched inside the palace. Ben couldn't see, but heard the gates swing shut and lock.

Judgment

At the palace, Nathan Adamson was marched into the presence of Adam Chata. No trumpets, no drums, marked Nathan's advance, only the deadly rhythm of marching feet echoing on the cold stone floor of the judgment hall.

The judgment hall was a vast chamber designed to awe its victims by its sheer size alone. One hundred yards wide, two hundred yards long, and a ceiling so high it couldn't be properly discerned. The entrance was a towering arch, with twelve-foot wooden doors, each a foot thick. They swung open inwardly with ease, in total silence. Getting in was easy. Getting out again . . . . Only the Governor knew.

The room was half-lit, indicating to all who entered the darkness in which they moved. Only the high seat, the judgment seat, was fully illuminated. Those brought before it moved from shadow to light to have their deeds exposed and judged. It was not a place used for common crimes. Nothing save the severest of judgments were issued from the high seat.

The seat itself was a massive piece of highly polished cold stone, black as night, black as death. Its angles were sharp and unyielding, unadorned with curves or flourishes. No mercy existed here, only judgment. Indeed, judgment had already been determined before anyone was brought into the judgment hall. There was no further appeal, no petition possible when one faced the high seat, only a fearful look forward to the inevitable judgment.

The regiment marched the shackled prisoner to the

edge of the light, then dropped back into the gloom. Nathan and Athariym were left alone to face Adam Chata.

The hall had been cleared, and the governor sat enthroned in the high seat. His judgment robe shimmered in the intense light. Athariym paced nervously back and forth and began outlining his plan for his master. Periodically he would glance up at Chata to see if the governor were listening, or what reaction might be forthcoming. For nearly fifteen minutes he talked and there was no response. Athariym felt a sense of desperation as he finished. "So you see, sir, all we have to do is wait. I have ordered the messengers to stand by for an important announcement. If Ben doesn't show up in the next half hour, then we carry out the execution of the Chasidim leaders in the morning. People will know we're serious and will return Ben. And if they don't, well, then we will have eliminated the Chasidim once and for all. And if Ramah should happen to come forward, we can say that he has sold out to the enemy and can be eliminated with the rest of the traitors. Either way, we win."

Adam Chata waited until Athariym was finished, then addressed a question to Nathan. "What do you think? Have 'we' won?"

The emphasis on the word *we* caught Nathan's attention. He wondered if Athariym had caught it, as well. Evidently not. The young man was still trying to maintain a show of pride and confidence. Nathan remained silent. Athariym knocked Nathan's shoulder roughly. "The governor asked you a question. Answer him."

Nathan fixed his eyes on the governor. It was a strain; one eye was swollen completely closed, the other was blurry. Standing straight was painful, but Nathan was determined. His left side throbbed from repeated staff-butts, his right knee was severely twisted, if not broken altogether. It never occurred to Nathan that the sudden appearance, then disappearance of the soldier's quarry,

Kadosh Neshamah, would so enrage them. Nathan had become an open target for all their anger, frustration, and malice. Though Nathan had surrendered without a struggle, the soldiers had battered him more thoroughly than if he'd put up a fight. The earliest followers of Haben Jah had rejoiced that they were found worthy to suffer for Him. Nathan understood their feelings a little better now.

Athariym shoved Nathan again. "Answer him." Haben's words from the Kathab repeated in his head "And you will be brought before governors for My sake, for a testimony against them . . . . " Nathan found comfort in it, and said evenly, "We win."

Athariym missed the connection. Adam Chata didn't. The governor laughed harshly. "I see. The plan is to your liking, then?"

"No. But we win, anyhow."

Athariym stared at Nathan. He asked angrily, "What are you talking about? Who wins?" Nathan remained silent. Athariym struck the man hard in the face. "Answer me!"

Nathan tasted blood on his lip but remained silent. He rehearsed verses silently ". . . who, when He was reviled, reviled not again; when He suffered, He threatened not, but committed Himself to Him that judges righteously."

Athariym struck Nathan again. Adam Chata said, his voice bored, "Leave him alone, Athariym. I know his answer." The governor sighed deeply, then said, "So, we have won a major victory. The death of the Chasidim leaders, the virtual elimination of their followers, and the removal of Ben Ramah from power. Is that how you see it?"

"Oh, yes sir."

"Uh huh. And what of this pathetic figure here? You have spread the rumor that Neshamah has been captured. You can sell that to the masses, but not for long."

Athariym looked perplexed. "What do you mean, sir?"

He looked at Nathan. "If we have the Chasidim, we have Neshamah. He cannot operate without them."

Nathan couldn't help it. He smiled slightly. Adam Chata glared at the hapless young man. "Get out, you fool! Get out. Leave me to redeem this worthless mess you have created."

Athariym was completely bewildered. "But sir, . . . I don't understand."

"Out!" Chata roared in frustration. Athariym fled the chamber, leaving Nathan alone with the governor. Adam Chata paced slowly in front of Nathan. "You see the difficulties I must face, overseeing a flock of idiots and fools."

Nathan bit back the jibe on his tongue and remained silent. Chata continued, "He has told the world Kadosh Neshamah is captured. He intends to parade you as Neshamah, no doubt." Nathan shrugged but said nothing. Chata continued, "An admirable plan but hardly feasible. Still, it might be made to work, with a little cooperation." The governor eyed Nathan. "An exchange of mutual benefit, perhaps. You claim to be Neshamah, I release your three friends."

Nathan rolled his eyes in disgust. Chata chuckled. "Of course not. That's too simple. And besides, your friends have made their decisions. They will stand by their 'truth' regardless." Chata smiled, "But perhaps if the stakes were more personal. And higher?"

Nathan felt a chill run through him. He eyed the governor closely. Chata noted the change in Nathan's expression and nodded. "Ah, so you can be reached. You do have a price."

Nathan said flatly, "I have no price."

Chata shrugged. "You did once before."

The nightmare vision of his betrayal of his wife flashed through Nathan's mind. *Yaldah, dear Yaldah!* She had become a follower of Haben Jah two years after they were married, one year before Rachel was born. Nathan was a man on the move, then, a minor government advisor working his way to the top. He hadn't lied to Ben Ramah when he said he saw himself in Ben. It was far too true for comfort. Nathan had considered separating from Yaldah at the time. He would have been fully within his rights to do so. But for all his self-seeking, he couldn't do it. He loved her too much to divorce her.

But not enough to save her. Nathan managed to cover Yaldah's unfortunate allegiance to Haben Jah for nearly eight years. Rachel was six, Jonathan four, when Nathan was nominated for the position of prime minister. It was the job he'd worked, sweated, bled, and cried for all the years in service. His for the taking, if . . . .

If he would denounce Yaldah once and for all. The new prime minister could afford no taint on his reputation, no hint of disloyalty, nothing but absolute and total commitment to Governor Chata and his reforms. The choice was clear and irrevocable. Denounce Yaldah as a Habenist, and he could continue in public office. Rachel and Jonathan were included in his offer, a rational "out" to clear his conscience, if he still had one. Denouncing Yaldah would allow him to retain custody and control of the children. If he chose not to, well, he would keep his children, to be sure. But there would be none of the elite schools, none of the opportunities that only the truly privileged enjoyed.

Nathan hadn't taken long to decide. And though it pained him some, he uttered the fateful words that sent Yaldah away; to her death, he now knew. "I denounce Yaldah and all she believes. I do not serve Haben Jah as she does. I serve only myself."

Back in the judgment hall, Nathan addressed Adam Chata, "That was a long time ago, I know better now. I know Haben Jah now."

Adam Chata smiled again. "Ah, yes, you do know Him don't you? And therefore your destiny is secure, so you believe. Anything I can do to you is merely a reward and puts you closer to your Lord. Isn't that it?"

Nathan quoted, " 'In God have I put my trust, I will not fear what men can do to me.' "

Chata nodded. "Of course, of course." The governor paced slowly around Nathan; as though considering his options. Nathan watched him closely, the chill still on him.

Chata stopped pacing and smiled again. "Well enough for you, I suppose. But what of those less secure in their allegiances? Let's say, for example, oh . . . your daughter Rachel. Better yet, your son, Jonathan. Do you suppose he would be so trusting?"

Nathan's stomach wrenched, and his eyes betrayed him. Jon . . . not Jon.

Chata beamed with glee. "Ah, yes, you do see my point, don't you? While your eternal destiny is not in question, your son's is. Were he to die, now, unconverted as you say, where would he be?"

Nathan took a long, deep breath and let it out slowly. He studied the face of his tormentor, all the while praying silently. Chata smiled patiently, waiting for Nathan's response. The governor added, "Oh, and lest you think he is beyond my reach, let me assure you I have servants in Yada as well. Some of them have already made contact with your son. If you are wondering, he is more opposed to Haben Jah than he was when you first took him to Yada."

Adam Chata smiled. "Watch and see." The Governor clapped his hands sharply. The room went completely dark. Chata's voice ordered, "Show us the son."

A dim glow appeared directly in front of Nathan. Nathan closed his eyes quickly. Use of divination and the ancient magic was strictly forbidden in the Kathab. One relied on Haben Jah for wisdom, never on the occult. Its use was a snare and a cheat, and Nathan had to avoid it all costs. He whispered, "Lord Haben Jah . . . ." but stopped as a familiar voice, so like his own, said, "I hoped this place could do better than just a daydream."

"It can. Indeed it can. Sha'a has the ability to give substance to your dreams."

Nathan's eyes opened and his heart stopped. Jonathan, his son, his child, was in Sha'a. Sha'a, city of delights, so far off the path to Amanah that few who went there ever returned. Or wanted to return. *Jon, Jon, what are you doing?*

Nathan watched in horror as Jon began to live out his fantasy of being Governor of Golah. He was going to eliminate the Chasidim once and for all. Jon was imagining himself sitting in the Governor's seat overlooking the central square in Tebel-Ayr. Jon surveyed the ragged mob below. Men, women, children, all staring at him, knowing his next word would mean life or death for them. Jon let the glow of his incredible power fill every corner of his being. His power, his alone. He was in command. With one word he could destroy them all. Nathan could not only see the vision as Jon saw it, but felt the intoxication his son was experiencing. Jon raised his hand, smiling malevolently at the masses below him. It would be so simple. And not one person would dare oppose him. So simple . . . .

The vision faded, leaving Nathan alone and empty. Though he knew in his head the vision was a cheat, he also knew there was truth in its depiction of his son. What he saw was either truly happening, or would happen, or had already happened. Worse was the realization that it might happen if Nathan made the wrong choice. *Jon, my son, my* son.

Nathan's heart burned within his, as only a parent's can. The light returned to shine on Adam Chata. Chata's voice became cold and threatening. "Your feeble attempt to rescue him has failed, Adamson. He is mine. Unless you agree to help me, he will die. And be mine throughout eternity." The governor's eyes glittered malevolently. "I win."

Nathan continued to face Chata, silent, aching, and unsure. Chata smiled again, benevolence returning. "Give it some thought, Adamson. Take your time. I'll give you, oh, say, fifteen minutes or so. That ought to about do it. Let me know what you decide." Chata stepped down from the judgment seat and clasped his hand strongly on Nathan's shoulder, as if in deepest respect and friendship. "I'm sure we can reach an agreement." He winked at Nathan, then called, "Guard." Two soldiers stepped forward. Nathan wasn't sure if they had been standing there during his ordeal. "Take my guest to the holding area. He has an important decision to make. Be sure he is comfortable." He nodded to Nathan, "After you've made your decision, we can tend to those wounds. They need to be looked at, you know. I'll see you shortly. Till then."

He motioned for the soldier; the man caught Nathan's arm and led him away. Chata waited until they were gone, then smiled contentedly to himself. He strutted back to his judgment seat, sat down, and beamed happily. He whispered again, "I win."

Ben paced nervously outside the palace grounds, watching anxiously for any sign of guards. Had his messages gotten through? Dabar had to see him. He owed Ben, and they both knew it. That unfortunate incident at the pleasure house; Ben had helped cover it over. The victim's family had been amply compensated out of Ben's own pocket. No word ever reached the masses about the prime minister's indiscretion. Ben had never collected on the debt—until now. Surely Dabar would see him. He had to. He had to.

Ben paced a few more precious minutes, then stopped angrily. Dabar wasn't coming. That was obvious. Athariym's story was working. If Ben was labeled a traitor or, at the very least, under the influence of the Chasidim, then nothing he said would be held as credible. He still had his proofs, but they rested in the safe in his office. Trying to reach his office would be futile. Doubtless Athariym was inhabiting it.

So much for his carefully gathered intelligence. Well, there were other ways and means to accomplish the same ends. If those who could be blackmailed were inaccessible, those who could be bought weren't. Batsa came to mind immediately. Always for sale to the highest bidder, Ben could count on his cooperation. As long as the money held out. But that created new problems. Batsa was strictly a "cash and carry" customer. Ben had no way of getting his money.

Ben sighed and headed away from the palace. There had to be a way to rescue Nathan Adamson. Ben would not have the man die thinking Ben had betrayed him. Besides that, Ben had too many questions yet to ask him. There had to be a way.

Lost in thought, Ben was unaware his steps were following familiar pathways. It wasn't until he heard a gasp of, "It's him! It's Ramah!" that he looked up. In sudden fear he realized he'd walked into the guard station at the front of the palace. A guard grabbed for him. Ben jerked away and ran back out the door. The soldier shouted, "Get him! After him, quick!"

Ben dashed behind the wall, turned a corner, and ran directly into a relief detachment. Someone shouted; Ben crashed to the left and raced desperately across the palace grounds. No thought of direction prompted him, only the animal instinct to *run*. His pursuers pounded closer behind him. It was futile, he knew. They were rigorously trained; he was an out-of-shape diplomat. Still, he kept running, turning corners, dashing left and right, trying to shake them off. His feet seemed to have a destination of their own, one Ben knew nothing about. All he knew was to stop was death, to run was life. Or a chance, anyhow. But how long could he go? His side ached and his chest burned with pain. He was breathing in sharp, ragged gasps. It was useless. He couldn't win. In desperation he choked, "Help me, please. Help me." He rounded another corner and stopped dead in shock.

Haben Jah stood before him. Ben recognized the face, even though he'd never seen his former enemy before. Ben hesitated only a moment, then raced to the Man. He gasped, "Help me. I'll do anything, anything, at all if You'll help me. I was wrong, before. I'm sorry."

Haben Jah stared silently at Ben, His face unreadable. Ben searched His eyes, trying to catch some glimmer of meaning in them. He could hear the guards pounding closer. Ben dropped to his knees and begged, "Please. I'm sorry. I'll do anything if You'll save me, now."

Haben Jah smiled sadly. A look of compassion, tinged with sorrow came on His face. He said quietly, "So you say. Rise. These pursuers will not come near you."

Unsure of what to do, or what to expect, Ben got up slowly and looked behind him. The soldiers were approaching rapidly. The first guard ran to where Ben stood and kept right on running. A second followed suit. So did the third, and the fourth, and the fifth. Ten soldiers ran directly in front of Ben and never missed a step. All passed him without stopping.

Ben's eyes grew wide with fear. He faced Haben Jah and whispered, "My God."

Haben shook His head, "You do not yet mean that as you ought. Go back to Leah Bataqab. She is waiting for you."

"Leah? She's changed her mind? How?"

Haben Jah repeated His command, "Go back to Leah."

Before Ben's eyes the Man vanished. Ben stared in awe and fear, confused and unsure. What had just happened? What . . . ?

Ben looked around slowly. No trace of his pursuers remained; he was alone. Now what? Where could he go? What should he do?

Go to Leah Bataqab, the thought repeated in his head. But that made no sense. She'd thrown him out before. Why would . . . .

Go to Leah. The thought came, more forcefully this time.

Ben muttered, "All right, all right. I'll go. I said I'd do anything." Ah, but did he know what "anything" really meant? Ben began walking slowly across town. He was about to find out, wasn't he? Firsthand, up close, and personal. This could be more than he bargained for. Time would tell. Ben walked on.

Daniel sat cross-legged on the floor of his bedroom, the Kathab on his lap. Ruth entered; Daniel looked up at her. She smiled but her soft brown eyes held a look of tender concern. Daniel studied his wife a moment. Childbearing had added a good many pounds to her pleasantly full frame, pounds he knew she despaired of ever losing. Daniel was secretly convinced that the pounds would melt away once the twins began running in opposite directions. He had no illusions that raising twins would be easy. Evidently Ruth had the same opinion. She had cut her rich black hair just before the babies were born, forsaking the length Daniel loved for the expediency of short, quick, and easy to ignore. A wise woman.

Ruth sat down beside Daniel and gave him a warm hug. "You've been in here all evening. I worry about you. What can I do?"

Daniel shook his head. "I don't know, Ruth." He returned her embrace. "I've been praying and praying for an answer, for some direction to go. I feel totally helpless against Adam Chata, but I know I have to do something. The answers just aren't coming, Ruth, and I don't understand it."

Ruth eyed her husband silently. Daniel knew the look and asked, "What is it? What am I missing?"

Ruth considered her words carefully, then said gently,

"Maybe what you need isn't inspiration, my love. Maybe it's application."

"What?" Daniel was confused.

Ruth tried to explain. "Haben Jah is the Word, the Living Word. The Kathab is His written Word."

"I know that."

Ruth sensed his impatience. "Follow, Daniel. Within the Kathab are two Words. The Logos is all of Scripture, cover to cover. The rhema is a set of specific instructions for a particular situation or circumstance. You have a problem: what do you do about Adam Chata? Have you searched for what Haben Jah has already told us to do about a corrupt, evil government?"

Daniel shook his head. "It's not just the Governor. It's Arek and the others. What do I do for them?"

"Weren't there examples given of Haben's followers who were arrested and threatened? What did Haben say His people did? That's what I'm talking about." Ruth kept her words gentle. "It's too easy to sit and wait for answers to fall from the sky, dear heart. We get to be lazy disciples, that way. The King gave us wisdom." She patted the Kathab lovingly. "He expects us to use it. Then if we still lack wisdom, we can ask."

Daniel smiled, in spite of himself. He kissed Ruth lightly on her head and asked, "How do you know these things?"

Ruth's eyes glowed. "Haben taught me."

"I see." Daniel picked up the Kathab. "And so, if I asked you where to look for those specific instructions you could tell me where they were."

Ruth nodded. "I could. But I won't. You need to search it out on your own. Otherwise I might give you only that part of the answer that I want you to see. 'All Scripture is given by God, and is profitable . . .' but only if you use all Scripture."

Daniel nodded, stood up stiffly, then helped Ruth to her

feet. "We'd better go to the table. This could be a long study."

Ruth smiled.

Nathan sat warily on the floor in the holding area. The room was empty, without windows or furnishings of any kind. Light filtered in through the ceiling. Nathan had no sense of time and didn't know whether fifteen minutes or fifteen hours had passed. All he knew was he was alone.

No, not alone. *I will never leave you, nor forsake you. Lo, I am with you 'til the end of the age* . . . .

Nathan sighed slightly, then said, "Direct me, Haben."

"I have."

Neshamah stood before Nathan. Nathan looked at his Guide and asked, "What do I do? Jon . . . ."

"Jon is in the Hands of the King, Nathan. You placed him there. Are you now going to withdraw him?"

Nathan shook his head. "No, of course not."

"The issue of his salvation was predetermined from the foundations of the world. Can you alter that by bargaining with Adam Chata?"

Again Nathan shook his head. "No."

"Then what choice will you make?"

Nathan dropped his eyes. *Yes, but* rang in his head. "Yes, but I can save him." "Yes, but You don't know Jon like I do." "Yes, but this is different . . . ." A thousand "yes, buts" did not alter the reality of the King's sovereign will. Nathan waited for the turmoil inside to scream its last protest, then looked up. He stared steadily into the face of Neshamah and said, "I will make no bargains. I will never deny Haben Jah."

Neshamah smiled. "Well done, Ben-'el. Be of good courage. Delight yourself in the Lord, and He will give you the desire of your heart."

"I will." Faith restored, Nathan nodded. "I will."

Neshamah disappeared. The door opened; two soldiers entered. One stood guard, the other helped Nathan to his feet. Roughly he forced the man out the door, down the corridor, and back to the audience chamber.

Arek, Ahab, and Chedvah stood silently on one side of the room, shackled and bound. Athariym paced nervously back and forth in front of the judgment seat. Nathan was led to a place opposite the Chasidim leaders. He acknowledged the elders with a nod; they nodded in return. All was settled.

Ten minutes passed. Athariym glanced anxiously at the guard and demanded, "Where is the Governor? What's keeping him?"

The guard shrugged. "He ordered us to bring the prisoners here, and then to wait. I follow orders, sir."

Athariym snarled lowly, but didn't comment. He resumed his pacing.

Another ten minutes passed. Athariym muttered, "We're past my deadline. This won't work. If the people don't believe we're serious, this won't work at all." The young man looked at the guard. "Go find the Governor. Tell him . . . ."

The guard shook his head. "No, sir, I won't. I have my orders. They were to bring the prisoners here and then to wait. I will not go beyond that."

Athariym snapped, "Then I'll find him." He stalked to the door but found the exit blocked by two soldiers. He ordered fiercely, "Get out of my way."

Neither soldier moved. One said, "Orders, sir. No one is to leave. You are to wait with the others."

Athariym exploded. "What? This is ridiculous? Get out of my way!"

The soldiers dropped their staffs across the door; Athariym froze. The guard repeated coldly, "You are to wait with the others."

Athariym hesitated, then walked back to the front of the chamber. Nathan's eyes twinkled. He shouldn't enjoy the youngster's discomfort, but he did. There was such a thing as righteous vengeance. This wasn't it, but Nathan couldn't help enjoying the moment. The spoiler becoming the spoiled. Yes, there was justice to be had in this hall.

Leah painted with rough, jerky strokes. Her landscape had become so abstract not even she could discern its features. She glanced again at the street, anxiously waiting. It was useless to look. Evening lay heavily on the city of Tebel-Ayr. The night looked darker than it ever had before. Dark night for dark deeds.

Where was Ramah? Why hadn't he come? Neshamah said he would, so where was he? Mirmah's messengers had spread the word, and though no one had seen Ramah, it was known everywhere he was headed this way. So where was he? Mirmah was securely hidden in the back room. He had left earlier but returned shortly after the dinner hour. He would be getting impatient, too. Where *was* Ramah?

Leah dabbed absently at her paints but missed the container. She pulled back sharply and upset the entire easel. Painting and paints crashed to the floor. She kicked angrily at the offending easel, sending it skidding across the floor. The painting left a crimson trail before it came to rest against the far wall. Leah stared at the mess, breathing hard. She had to get herself under control. If Ramah sensed her anxiety, he'd never trust her . . . .

Trust her so she could betray him. Leah closed her eyes tightly and shook her head. For Arek. All this was for Arek. Revenge had nothing to do with it. It didn't. It didn't. It was all to rescue Arek.

Leah drew a slow breath, let it out slowly, and felt control returning. She glanced back down the street. Still no sign. She should clean up the mess before the paint stained. She bent over and set the pots upright. It would be necessary to replace the white. Hard to come by, true, pure white paint, these days. Everything had a gray tinge to it, it seemed. Leah wiped up as much paint as she could with her smock, then went to the kitchen for a rag. As she opened the door, she stopped cold. "You!"

Ben Ramah stood quietly, watching her. Neither spoke for several moments. Finally, Ben said, "I didn't turn Adamson in."

Leah dropped her eyes and nodded. "I know." She looked around the kitchen, grabbed a towel from the counter, and walked back to the painting. Ben followed her. Leah knelt down and dabbed at the remaining stains.

Ben hesitated, then said, "Leah . . . ." She looked up. The man struggled with the words. "I . . . I want to help. I don't know how, but I want to help."

Leah stared at him in fascination. "You mean that, don't you?"

"I do."

"Why?"

Ben shook his head. "I can't explain it. But I have to do something, anything, to get Adamson free."

Leah looked back at the floor quickly. This wasn't the Ben Ramah she'd expected. She scrubbed harder at the painted floor, then suggested softly, "You could turn yourself in."

Ben nodded. "I'd thought about that." Leah's head jerked up in surprise. Ben nodded again. "I did. But I know Adam Chata too well. He won't bargain. He might say he will, but he won't."

Leah looked back at the floor. "How do you know? It's worth a try, isn't it?"

Ben shook his head, "It's not. It's a worthless gesture. Adam Chata would never release Adamson now that he holds him. If I walked in there, he'd throw me, Adamson, and your friends all together as conspirators, and we'd all die."

Leah said, "I never said just walk in. But the offer could be made, you know; free the Chasidim and I'll come in."

"It sounds good. But you don't know the man like I do,

Leah. I've worked for him too long to believe he'd go for it."

Leah heard frustration in Ben's voice. She stole a glance at his face and saw desperation in his eyes. Ben Ramah, desperate? But then, Ben Ramah, wanting to help someone else? Leah said slowly, "I think it's worth a try." She looked Ben full in the face and said, "I think it can work. I think Adam Chata can be made to bargain, if the deal is sweet enough." She raised her voice and called sharply, "Mirmah!"

Mirmah burst from the back room and grabbed for Ben. Ben ducked, but Mirmah lunged again and knocked him against the wall. Ben instinctively swung at his attacker. Mirmah caught the blow on his shoulder, then delivered his own punch to Ben's waist. Ben doubled over in pain. Mirmah struck him hard in the face, pinning him to the wall. Mirmah raised his fist to strike again, but Leah ordered sharply, "Enough! Mirmah, stop!"

Mirmah held his punch but complained, "I'm not finished yet."

"Yes, you are." Leah got up from the floor and walked over to the corner where Ben lay. She pulled Mirmah back and stared at her enemy.

Ben looked up at her but said nothing. The look in his eyes, though . . . Leah's voice shook as she said, "It will work, Ben. I can make it work." Ben turned his head away. Leah motioned to Mirmah. "Take him to the council room at the Bavith. Hold him there." She ordered sternly, "Don't hurt him anymore. Just keep him there, until I send for you."

Mirmah smiled, "My pleasure." He caught Ben's arm and roughly dragged the man out the back door.

Leah's Dilemma

Leah waited until they were gone, then sighed bitterly. She thrust the memory of the look in Ben's eyes away and steeled herself for the task ahead. It wouldn't do to ask audience with Chata dressed in a paint rag. She changed quickly into the one ceremonial gown she owned. As niece to Nadiyb Bataqab, she enjoyed much of his authority and position. She'd never exercised it before, but the right was there. Now was the time to use it, to find out if being a princess of the 'Ibriy held any true value. Leah muttered, "Uncle Nadiyb, you always said the name Bataqab carried weight. You had better be right. Just this once, I hope you are right." Leah pinned the kiymah to her shoulder, nodded curtly to her reflection, and headed out the door.

Leah walked quickly across town. Mirmah had told her of the night's deadline; it was nearly time. There was no way she could make it to the palace before then, not on foot. The swiftest messenger couldn't get there from here. There was only one way she knew of, a way disapproved and rejected by her people from time out of mind. But right now, it didn't matter. The end justified all means, didn't it? Didn't it?

Leah swallowed hard and kept walking. It did. She'd repent later. Besides, who was going to know? Leah closed her eyes and summoned one of the ravens. She'd learned how in school, long ago, from a friend. She'd also been punished severely by her parents for doing it. But she'd never quite forgotten how. And the idea of using Adam

Chata's own weapons against him was in its own way appealing. Almost instantly there was a rustle of wings. A huge raven landed beside her. He cocked his head and waited. Leah ordered, "Raven, carry this message to your master. Tell him one who has Ramah seeks audience with him. Tell him not to harm the Chasidim, and to wait. Much that he desires can be had with patience. Go swiftly and deliver the message." The raven squawked, launched itself into the air, and was gone.

Leah nodded to herself and quickened her pace. She wondered briefly what it was she could offer Adam Chata but did not linger over the matter. She was sure all would be made clear, later. So far, her plan was working.

Leah arrived at the palace the same time Nathan Adamson and the others were being brought into the judgment hall. She had no way of knowing and could only hope her message had been received. As she approached the gates, the ceremonial guard snapped to attention. He saluted her and said curtly, "His eminence, Governor Chata, extends his warmest regards to the Princess Bata-qab. I am to escort you to the hall of audiences where our Governor will gladly receive the offer of friendship you bring."

Leah bit her tongue, then said, "Very good. Lead on." As she fell in step behind the guard, she breathed a small sigh of relief and triumph. So, her message had gotten through. So much for step one. Now, step two. Making an offer Adam Chata wouldn't refuse outright. Better, making an offer he would accept outright. The undying friendship and devotion of the 'Ibriy? Too tall an order. Her firstborn male child? Hardly. Then again, since she intended to remain single the rest of her life . . . No, not feasible. Besides, she'd never wish Adam Chata on any child. How about . . . the head of Ben Ramah on a platter? She was giving him that, anyhow. Maybe it would be enough. So far, all she had was Ramah's word it wouldn't. What did he know? He was probably too self-seeking to try it. Leah encouraged herself down the long, silent corridors that led to the hall of audiences. It would work. She'd make it work.

Two of the palace guards stood watch outside the hall. They came to attention as Leah's escort approached. One opened the massive doors, which swung silently inward, admitting Leah into the very presence of Adam Chata, Governor of Golah.

The hall itself was barren of adornments. Floors and walls were of the same highly polished material as the wall around the city, though of a much lighter hue. The room seemed to sparkle, as every light source was caught, reflected, and magnified one hundredfold.

Lanterns hung every ten feet to enhance the effect of dazzling brilliance. The room was narrow, only twelve feet across, but ran forty feet long. Chairs lined the walls, waiting for the most important of persons to fill them. Only the most honored guests greeted Adam Chata in this hall, and only on matters of the utmost importance.

Near the center of the hall was a long, rough-hewn stone table. It looked out of place amid the brilliance of the room itself. The contrast was deliberate. Three chairs had been carefully arranged; one on either side, one at the end. Leah knew the custom: the third chair stood for the unseen guest at every occasion. The 'Ibriy would say the King; the Chasidim would call Him Haben Jah. Others called it the 'life force' or simply 'God within.' No matter, really. They were all word games, weren't they?

Leah swallowed hard as she walked forward. Adam Chata was waiting for her at the table, smiling happily. He extended his hand in welcome and said warmly, "Come in, Your Highness. Come in. Such a pleasure to have you within these humble walls."

Leah forced herself to shake his hand in return, though she loathed the touch of his flesh. Adam Chata's grip was soft and clammy. Leah withdrew her hand as quickly as possible and sat down opposite the governor.

Chata continued to smile. "To what do I owe this delight?"

Leah cleared her throat and came straight to the point. "You are holding a friend of mine, Arek, of the Chasidim. I want to bargain for his freedom."

Chata looked amazed. "Arek of the Chasidim? He is a friend of the 'Ibriy?"

"No. He is a friend of mine. A personal friend. I want him released."

The governor frowned slightly. "That is a problem. Arek is being held on charges of conspiracy against this administration. Very serious charges, you realize."

Leah eyed the man carefully. "I know the charges are false. So do you. The charge was laid in order to find Ben Ramah, to force him out of hiding. I know where Ramah is and can produce him at will." She lifted her head slightly. "I want Arek. You want Ramah." She smiled. "Let's make a deal."

Chata chuckled. "I see. You, no doubt, have proof of your words."

Leah nodded, "No doubt." She offered nothing more. She was on dangerous ground and knew it. She should have brought something. How could she have overlooked so simple a thing as proof?

Chata merely shrugged. "May I see your proof?"

"In time." Now what? Leah countered, "You, no doubt, have proof Arek is alive. And well."

"No doubt."

The glint in Chata's eyes made Leah squirm inwardly. The man was no fool, and not a novice at this. Leah realized for the first time she was out of her league, dealing with an adversary far beyond her measure. She eyed Chata intently wondering what to do next. A verse from the songs of the son of Jesse came to her: "Trust in the Lord with all your heart, and lean not on your own understanding. In all your ways acknowledge Him, and He will direct your path." Good advice. A little late, perhaps, but worth a try. Leah prayed silently, 'Lord King, direct me now. Show me how to bargain with this man."

There was no answer; only silence. Leah looked at Adam Chata and asked, "May I see Arek?" Inwardly she called again, 'Lord King, hear me. Answer me. What do I do?"

Chata shook his head. "Not at this time. You have my word he is alive. And well." The governor smiled. "And since we are both honest, righteous citizens of Golah, our words may be trusted implicitly. True?"

Leah read the sarcasm and knew she'd been trapped. She prayed in desperation, 'Neshamah, help me. Lead me in how to make this deal work. I want Arek free. Help me."

But silence was still the answer. Leah knew why. Having leaned on her own understanding to begin this course of action, how could she expect the King to sanction it by bringing it to pass? She'd disobeyed Him to start with and now wanted Him to bail her out. And on *her* terms, no less. The lesson struck home. Leah looked back into the eyes of Adam Chata, swallowed hard, and said, "No doubt." She hesitated only slightly, then forged ahead. "This is what I propose."

Mirmah shoved Ben Ramah roughly into the council chamber room at the Bavith. The council would not meet again for three months; the room would be empty until then. Ben made a last attempt at resistance, lunging at his captor in desperation. Mirmah sidestepped the rush, then lashed out, kicking Ben's legs out from under him. Ramah crashed hard to the floor. Mirmah aimed a sharp kick at the man's head but stopped short. He laughed harshly and said, "You're not worth the trouble. I'm sure your governor will devise reward enough for you."

Mirmah turned and walked out the door, slamming it hard. Ben heard the tumblers click, knew it was locked, but felt compelled to try it anyhow. He struggled to his feet, staggered to the door, and attempted to turn the handle. Locked. Ben tugged vainly on the door, but it didn't give. He turned and sagged against it, trying to catch his breath and force himself to think. He looked around the room for inspiration but found none. Paneled in rich cedar, the room was empty of furniture, windows, or exits, save the one behind him. Light beamed through the ceiling glass. If he could get to the ceiling, he could break the glass and get out. But how to reach the ceiling?

Ben felt overwhelmed. He saw no way out. Ben wasn't ready to give up and he wasn't thinking about suicide, no matter what the New Order taught about the glories of the next life. Especially now. Especially if what Nathan Adamson, the Chasidim, and the Kathab all said were true. He'd never believed it before. But he'd never faced Kadosh Neshamah—much less Haben Jah Himself—before. Not that seeing Them had made his life any easier. Quite the opposite, in fact.

So what to do? Ben sank down uncomfortably and sat on the floor. He needed help, that was obvious. But whom could he trust? His family members were highly placed and loyal government figures. They would not jeopardize their own positions to rescue him. Friends? He had none. None that could be counted on to help. So what could he do?

Ben shook his head angrily. He was thinking in circles, getting nowhere. Maybe it was time to get back to what he knew. Creative visualization. Call Kechash 'owb, let him figure a way out. Worth a try, anyhow. Ben closed his eyes and chanted softly.

Nothing happened. Confused, Ben tried again. Still nothing. There was only darkness and emptiness within. No tunnel, no light, no welcoming guide . . . only blankness. With a sinking feeling of total dejection, Ben realized he'd been shut out. For the first time in his conscious life, he was totally alone.

Ben stared blankly at the floor. Why? Why was this

happening? He was the one with all the control, his life neatly ordered and organized. What had gone wrong?

Haben Jah, that's what. In seeking to learn the truth about Haben Jah, his world had been turned upside down. No mere myth could disrupt a life so. And the Man who he'd run to on the street . . . that had been no myth. Adamson had said the heart of the matter was Haben Jah. Who was He, really?

Ben pulled the satchel he carried over his shoulder and took the Kathab from it. Mirmah hadn't bothered to confiscate it with Ben's other belongings. He hadn't paid any attention to it; almost as if he he hadn't even seen it. Like the soldiers hadn't seen him. Ben picked the Kathab up carefully and found the section Nathan Adamson had recommended. It started with the birth of Haben Jah. Ben read aloud, "In the beginning was the Word. And the Word was with God, and the Word was God . . . and the Word became flesh and lived among us . . . ." Ben's voice trailed off. He read the words silently again, then looked up reflectively. He was Who? Ben looked back at the page and began reading again.

It took nearly two hours to work out the details of Ben Ramah's transfer and Arek's release to the mutual satisfaction of both Adam Chata and Leah Bataqab. Adam Chata smiled as the meeting concluded, and once again extended his hand to Leah. "A true pleasure doing business with a woman of vision such as yourself, Your Highness. I foresee a long and fruitful relationship for your people and my administration. Thank you for your cooperation."

Leah shook his hand curtly. The revulsion she'd felt at their first meeting was rekindled, but for different reasons. Then it had been at his touch; now, it was her own flesh that repelled her. Leah said, "We shall see. When all we have arranged comes to successful completion, then we shall see." She stood abruptly. "I must go. I have arrangements to make." Without awaiting permission or dismissal, Leah left the room. She held herself stiffly as she marched though the palace, out the doors, and past the gates. Only when she was out of sight of Biyrah did she sag noticeably. Leah walked to the nearest stone bench along the street and collapsed onto it. Unmindful of curious pedestrians, she buried her head in her hands and shut her eyes. What had she done?

Saved Arek. She'd saved Arek. But at what cost? Would Arek have approved? Of course not. He'd say the price was too high. But what did he know? This was all for him. The important thing was his life was to be spared. No matter that she'd compromised most all she held dear and sacred. She'd agreed to support Chata in his new reforms; agreed to lend her family name to help establish new training centers for displaced Chasidim, displaced by the new reforms, no doubt. She had agreed to sit in on the Governor's Council to lend credence to the new friendship between government and the 'Ibriy. And although she could not promise success, Leah had agreed to convince Arek and the others to soften their opposition to Chata. Neither the governor nor Leah believed it would happen, but the woman was to try, anyhow. And she was then to make full report of the Chasidim's response to Adam Chata's overtures of friendship.

What had she done? Given Chata everything he'd asked for, and more. Leah looked up slowly. Her stomach wrenched as she thought over the past two hours. She'd not only given him what he wanted, she'd even suggested additional ways she could assist Chata. Lord King, what had she done?

Saved Arek. Saved Arek? She'd gone far beyond that in bargaining. What had ever possessed . . . ?

Leah shuddered and stood up abruptly. No time for remorse now. She was to to bring Ramah to the town square. Chata was going to make the exchange in a very public place, before a very public public. Leah had no idea why Chata agreed so readily, happily in fact, to her demand for an open swap. No doubt, he had ulterior motives. Fine, as long as Arek came out alive and free. The woman set her shoulders and marched towards the Bavith. Mirmah would have to hold Ramah until the three leaders had been brought out. Chata was to make a "small address to the people," then let the Chasidim go free. Leah would then present Chata with the traitor, Ben Ramah, and all would be well.

Except, of course, for Ben. Leah dodged the memory of the look in his eyes. There *had* been something different about him, though. What? What could make an impact on a wretch like Ramah? Maybe not what. Maybe who. Or Who.

Leah shook her head angrily. It didn't matter. Let him worry about that. Besides, if Ben really was under the influence of Neshamah and Haben Jah, then He could protect him. That was His job, not hers.

Leah's steps slowed as her mind continued to twist round itself. What if Ramah was to become one of the Chasidim? She'd sworn to protect them, to help them.

She muttered through clenched teeth. "Not Ramah. Never."

Why not?

Because of what he did to me, she thought angrily. *He used me, then dumped me.*

And was what she had done any different? An eye for an eye, perhaps? Which made her no better than her enemy. Worse, in fact. Ramah hadn't claimed to be one of the Chosen, living a life directed by the King. Leah did.

Leah stopped. All this was getting beyond her. It had seemed so clear and simple just a few hours ago. Now it was getting clouded. Clouded by mercy and compassion, traits of the King Himself—traits of His Son Haben Jah.

Leah stared at the ground, trying to make up her mind. Two paths lay before her. Unlike so many times before, she saw them clearly. One path led to the Bavith, to carry out her deal with Adam Chata; to sell her soul to accomplish her own end. Her end, not Arek's, not Adam Chata's, certainly not the King's. Her own end.

The second path was much less attractive. It was the path marked by obedience, by grace and not judgment, by faith and not the maneuverings of her own will. It accepted the leading of the King, eschewed evil and compromise, and set Ramah free. Which path would she follow?

Leah stared at the ground, not seeing the street, nor the marketplace, oblivious to everything around her. Which path would she take? It didn't matter who had taken the paths before her. Parents, uncle, brother, friends, enemies, family . . . none of them mattered. It wasn't a question of who or how many had followed which course. The question was: which would she choose?

Leah stood silently for nearly five minutes. She choked back a soft sob, brushed a tear from her eye, and began walking. She had decided. There was nothing for it now but to carry it out. Determination flooded her. The woman picked up her pace.

A full two hours passed before Adam Chata made his entrance to the judgment chamber. He came in unannounced, without guard or fanfare. His head was down, as if lost in thought. The Governor of Golah walked past his guests without taking any notice of their presence. He strolled to the high seat, sat down, and only then looked up. Then, as if with a start, he said, "Oh, gentlemen. Forgive me. I forgot you were waiting for me. I hope you'll excuse me. I have a matter of deep concern to settle."

Nathan eyed Ahab, waiting for the elder Chasidim to take the lead. Ahab shrugged. "No matter. Take all the time you need. We have all of eternity."

His stress on the word "we" did not go unregistered. Adam Chata said dryly, "Of course. I had forgotten."

Athariym was ready to explode. His impatience, coupled with what he saw as the failure of his carefully laid plans, pushed him to his limit. His voice was strangled as he asked, "Governor, sir, do you realize what you have done? By waiting you've shown the masses of Golah that your word is without value! You set a deadline for Ben Ramah's return. The fact that these men remain alive is proof you . . . ."

Athariym trailed off under the Governor's icy gaze. Adam Chata spaced his words carefully. "My word is law, Athariym. My word is life and light to this world. Whatever my word says is, is. If I choose to demonstrate mercy rather than execute justice, then that is my concern. The people of Golah understand how long-suffering I am; slow to anger and of great mercy. I am not willing that any should perish. Or don't you know that?"

Nathan winced inwardly at Chata's blasphemy but modeled his responses after the other leaders. Calm. The King Himself would one day restore descriptions to their rightful owners.

Chata relaxed slightly and continued, "Besides, Ben Ramah has returned."

Both Nathan and Athariym jerked in response. Athariym voiced the questions for Nathan. "What? How? When?"

Chata smiled. "Oh, he's not here, yet. But he will be, soon. I have assurances he will soon be brought in to me. At that time, I will have opportunity to finish this charade you so clumsily began." He surveyed the other occupants of the room and assured them, "You, too, my friends, will have a part in my production. Adamson, here, has already been shown the advantages of cooperating."

Nathan's eyes flashed. He started to object but a look from Ahab silenced him. Ahab said evenly, "We will do nothing but obey our Lord and King, Governor. That you know full well."

Adam Chata's eyes glinted. "I'm counting on it. Believe me, I am counting on it."

The Angel of Light

In a secluded inner chamber of the palace, Adam Chata meditated peacefully. His sanctuary was little more than a closet, four feet square, and not more than five feet high. Its walls were heavily draped to absorb any outside sounds. The floor, too, was thickly cushioned, both for sound and to provide comfort during the long hours the governor spent kneeling and praying, or sitting in the lotus position, meditating. It was not unheard of for Adam Chata to spend days in his chamber, refusing food, drink, and sleep, in pursuit of inner cleansing. His brightest and best reforms came after such purging. It was then he was most completely in contact with the angel of light who directed his path, providing the governor with wisdom and insights not otherwise available to the common man.

Exposing the myth of One Divine king had come from one such meditation. From his earliest childhood Adam Chata had heard of the King, creator of Heaven and Earth, ruler of the universe itself. Clothed in majesty and light, He reigned as supreme judge over all the earth. In Him was all glory and honor and power. And power was the one thing Adam Chata craved beyond all other passions. From infancy, through childhood, beyond his teen years and into adulthood. Adam Chata pursued power: power to direct his own life, to direct the lives of those around him, and ultimately, to direct the lives of all men everywhere.

The stories of the King said He promised to share His power with men, freely and completely, that they might be one with Him. "Joint-heirs," Chata was taught. But there was a catch. To reign with the King, one had to first surrender to Him, to bow the knee before Him, and acknowledge Him as Lord of all. The thought of kneeling before anyone other than himself was abhorrent to Chata. Surely there had to be another way to achieve the same end. He would search the universe if necessary to find it.

Adam Chata was only twenty when the answer finally came to him in a vision—an angel of light. His name was Heylel, and he knew the way to power without the King. Heylel told Chata that the King had lied. There was more than one way to share His glory. Humanity could finally be free from fear of judgment, free from any condemnation at all, when they understood that each person *was* the King. It was so simple, so beautiful. To kneel before the King was to kneel to yourself. Since the King created man in His image, the King existed within the heart and soul of each individual. All that needed to be known of the King could be found inside. No need for judgment, no need for salvation or a savior. Just be the god you are.

It was this vision Adam Chata began to share with the world, and thus began his rise to ultimate power. People didn't naturally realize their full potential as kings and gods; they had to be taught. Continually directed by Heylel, Adam Chata set about to recreate his world into the image of its creator. He was only slightly amazed at how readily his message was received, however. Heylel had told him thousands would throng to hear him if he followed the angel's course. He hadn't been wrong. All of Golah seemed desperate to shake off the bonds of the King and gladly flocked to Adam Chata's side. No King? No judgment? Every man free to do what was right in his own eyes? Paradise!

Only the Chasidim opposed him. The 'Ibriy disagreed with him, but tolerated his message. Oldest of the peoples of Golah, they had seen a countless succession of rulers and reformers come and go without major impact on them. Chata was just another face. So long as he left the 'Ibriy alone, let him do what he wanted. They would not actively support the Governor, but neither would they openly oppose him. Heylel cautioned Chata to maintain a hands-off approach with the 'Ibriy. They could be won in time.

The Chasidim were another story, however. They must be eliminated at all costs. They were the greatest challenge Adam Chata faced. Heylel hated and feared them above all, for the Chasidim knew him for who and what he really was: the King's sworn enemy. The Faithful maintained there was but One King, One Lord and Savior of all. And all who would come to the King must come to Him His way, believing in Haben Jah. The Chasidim proclaimed judgment was real, but could be escaped only through surrender to Haben Jah. Haben Jah: the King in human likeness, born as man to die for mankind, so mankind could live forever. But on His terms, not human terms.

The governor waited expectantly for inspiration to come. With so much ahead, he needed to be absolutely clear about the road he was taking. It was all truly beautiful. The final destruction of the Chasidim; the removal of Ben Ramah from power; the long-awaited marriage of his administration with the people of the 'Ibriy. How he had longed, labored, and lived for this day. And it was all coming to pass, just as the angel had foretold. Chata beamed happily. Yes, tomorrow would be a day to remember.

A radiant brilliance filled the room. Adam Chata bowed slightly before his lord and said joyfully, "It is happening as you said, lord. She agreed to it all. Soon the last opposition to your presence will be removed, and you can assume your rightful place again."

The light swirled excitedly. A voice spoke, low and strong. "You have done well, my son. Together, our efforts will bring to pass the final establishment of the New

Order. We will rule and reign as gods, for together we are god."

Chata nodded in solemn agreement. "Yes, lord."

The voice continued, "I was in the garden at the beginning of time, upon the holy mountain of God. I walked up and down in the midst of the stones of fire. I will be exalted once again, as at the first. We will be gods, as I promised Chavvah before."

Adam Chata nodded. Chavvah, mother of all mankind, had been the first to hear Heylel's message that there was another way to God except through obedience. Tempted by Heylel in the garden at the dawn of time, she had started mankind down the long road away from servitude to the King to service to oneself.

"You alone are worthy, lord."

"I am." The voice sounded a note of caution. "We must exercise care, however. The Enemy is strong and will seek to oppose us. We must move with utmost discretion. The woman must not suspect our plans for Arek and the others. They must be a willing sacrifice in order to set the example for their followers. They will, of course, choose death before betraying their Master. And that is what we want. Let it be abundantly clear to all who have ears to hear: the path of obedience is death. Honorable and righteous though it may be, it still provides us with the elimination of the last bastion of resistance."

Chata smiled. "It does, indeed. Brilliant, lord. Absolutely brilliant. A truly anointed plan."

The light swirled, increasing its radiance, and beamed with pride. "It is, indeed. I am the anointed cherub; all I do is brilliant."

Adam Chata bowed respectfully again. "This will be a moment in eternity; a moment to begin all other moments. The king has come into his own."

The light increased in intensity, until with a flash it disappeared. Adam Chata sat motionless a moment longer, allowing the full essence of the encounter to permeate his being. At last he rose, renewed and refreshed, and sauntered out of the chamber.

Two of Chata's elite guard stood silent watch. The governor smiled at the men, then directed one, "I have received a new vision and a new revelation. Send messengers throughout the city to proclaim the good news. Tomorrow, I will share the glad tidings with all who will listen. The faithful should assemble at the town square in the morning. Go swiftly now, and spread the word."

The guard saluted briskly and sprinted away down the hall. Adam Chata smiled at the remaining soldier. "Accompany me, son. I have much to attend to before morning. Much to attend."

"Yes, sir."

Adam Chata strolled off, whistling merrily.

Athariym paced nervously in the holding area. He'd been pacing ever since he and the Chasidim had been put there after their brief interview with Adam Chata, some three hours earlier. As his anxiety increased, so did his physical agitation. The young man was working himself into a frenzy.

Nathan Adamson watched the transformation with interest and a small measure of concern. He'd read in the Kathab of one so possessed: the demonic of Gadara had broken chains and fetters continually. In his present state, Athariym might be capable of reproducing the same feat. Nathan thought idly, *Maybe he'll tear the door off the hinges, and we can get out of here.*

Athariym showed no sign of attacking the door, however. He was more consumed with his pacing; up and down, up and down the twenty-foot length of room. Nathan wished the room had been as wide as it was long; Athariym could have had more room to roam. But the holding area was barely eight feet across. Nathan, Ahab and the other Chasidim had huddled at one end of the room, out of the line of fire, trying to give Athariym as much room as possible. They had given up trying to calm the young man; Athariym had merely snarled at their overtures. Instead, the men had spent the time praying for family, friends, brothers, and sisters in Haben Jah, as well as the situation at hand.

Nathan was surprised at how little time the others spent praying about the present circumstances. They were all far more concerned with strengthening their fellow laborers. Nathan had watched and listened during the prayer vigil and had learned much. The greatest lesson was that he still had a lot more to learn about serving Haben Jah.

Chedvah suggested, "We know the King inhabits the praises of His people. Let's begin thanking Him for where we are now."

Nathan glanced over at the leader in surprise. "Wait a minute. Thank Him for this? I don't understand. Haben Jah didn't cause this crisis. Adam Chata did."

Arek nodded. "So he did. But nothing happens in our life that hasn't been allowed or approved by the King Himself. The Kathab says, 'There shall no evil happen to the just.' Haben used a word there for evil that means nothingness, or uselessness. Nothing useless happens to us, Nathan. All of the Kathab is good for either doctrine, for reproof, for correction, or for instruction in righteousness. For those who follow Haben Jah, all of life falls into the same categories."

"You mean there can be a purpose in what's happening? No matter how bad it is?"

Arek nodded. "If there were no purpose, it wouldn't happen. No matter what Adam Chata or his lord, Heylel, may devise, it is the King Who determines the ultimate outcome. He is either sovereign or not. Either Lord of all or not Lord at all."

Nathan pondered this silently. A thousand, "But what abouts?" came to mind. He said slowly, "I see what you're saying, but . . . ." He shook his head. "But what about when innocent people suffer?"

Chedvah smiled slightly. "Brother Nathan, what is the key to understanding and pleasing our Lord?"

Nathan thought, then said, "Faith."

Chedvah nodded. "Without faith it is impossible to please Him. So it is written, and so it is. Faith says the Word is true, unfailing, and eternal. What the King said, He says now, and will say forever. You can't say 'I know what the Word says, but . . . .' There is no circumstance for which He did not plan or make provision." Chedvah smiled. "One of our brothers used to teach that he could not imagine the King sitting in Chayah saying, 'Oh, my, I didn't think of that one,' when a circumstance occurs in our lives. No, either it all applies, all the time, or none of it does."

Arek added, "There is a principle that says when experience and the Word appear to clash, cling to the Word. Eventually the experience will be revealed in its proper context within the Word."

Nathan studied for a moment, then admitted, "That's hard, sometimes."

"It may be. But let's try applying it now. We are in mortal danger; our lives hang in the balance. Family and friends have been threatened because of us. We are unsure of the future and concerned for those we love. How and what can we thank Haben Jah for, in all this?"

Ahab said quietly, "I am thankful we've been put together. 'Two are better than one; and a threefold cord is not quickly broken.' " He smiled. "Four is even better." He grew serious again. "If we had been separated and left alone, we could not as easily withstand Chata's devices."

Nathan said, "You mean I couldn't."

Arek shook his head. "None of us, Nathan. I am thankful for the opportunity we have to witness to those around us." He motioned towards Athariym, still pacing. "It may be that someone will see, hear, or come to understand because of what we are doing."

Chedvah added, "I'm thankful for this time we've had to pray." He grinned wryly, "Which of us would have taken three hours out of our day to lift up the concerns of our heart? 'Too busy,' we say. 'I would if I had time.' Well, I believe our Lord has given the time."

Nathan frowned. "You're not serious. You believe all of this was to give us time to pray?"

"Of course not. But we can be thankful for the opportunity. We can be thankful we know the One Who hears our prayers. We can be thankful we know the outcome, no matter what may happen in between." Chedvah nodded. "We can be thankful we have been chosen and not another. We can be thankful Haben Jah chose us to begin with and that He loves us, died for us, rose again for us, and now lives to pray for us." Chedvah's eyes sparkled. "And if Haben Jah stands before the King, praying for us, do you believe the King will say no to His son?"

Nathan smiled, finally, understanding at last. "No, He wouldn't."

"No, He would not, indeed. Adam Chata has no power over us. Not if we know and accept Haben Jah as Lord. It is only those who walk outside His will that need tremble." Chedvah motioned towards Athariym. "He holds his own future, and he knows it. In that, there is tremendous fear. But to know and trust One Who loves us to carry us; ah . . . ." Chedvah smiled widely, ". . . in that, is true peace. And joy."

Nathan said, "I see it now." He took a deep breath, then said, "I am thankful I had the chance to witness to Ramah. And may have the chance again, I don't know. But I am thankful for that."

Ahab smiled. "Very good, brother. Very good. Now, let's see what else there is." The men continued praying and praising.

Daniel and Ruth spent the evening in prayer and studying the Kathab. Daniel read and reread the accounts of the arrest of Haben Jah, looking for wisdom in what to do. He studied the lives of Haben's followers, to see how and what they did when they, too, were arrested, persecuted, threatened. He read the Kathab's instructions on how to deal with evil: overcome it with good. Submit to all authorities, knowing that no matter how corrupt they are, they are still instruments of the King, carrying out His will. Indeed, it was because of persecution that the message of Haben Jah was carried to the uttermost parts of the earth, as believers scattered and fled the Holy City. The King continually used the evil that men devised to bring good. How great a Lord we serve!

It was nearly midnight when Daniel finished his study. Ruth had worked with him, when she wasn't feeding babies, changing babies, feeding babies, changing babies, changing babies. . . . She had gone to bed perhaps an hour ago, trying to catch a couple of hours rest before the next round of feedings and changings. But Daniel had his answer. It wasn't the answer he wanted, perhaps, but he knew it was Haben's answer. Do nothing overt. No predawn rescue attempts, no storming the palace walls, no mass protests. No blackmailing his uncle, either. Wait. Pray. Pray fervently, pray continually, pray and be ready when Haben said to do otherwise. But for now, wait.

Daniel bowed his head. Keeping his voice low he said, "As You will, my Lord. Not my will, but Yours be done. I'll wait and pray. If there is more I can do, tell me and I'll do it. Thank You for not allowing me to run counter to Your plan." He smiled slightly. "Thank You for sending me to Shalom, and for her guidance. Thank You for her willingness to challenge me to study Your Word. Don't let me get so hard-hearted or stiff-necked that I fail to hear her, or You. I love You, Lord."

Daniel looked up and sighed contentedly. He yawned,

closed the Kathab and patted it tenderly. "Good night, Lord." In total peace he went and joined Ruth in bed. He climbed in, snuggled down beside her, and whispered, "Good night, Ruth. I think I can sleep now." He closed his eyes.

A baby began to cry. Daniel opened his eyes. Ah, round two. He shrugged. "Maybe I won't sleep. Maybe I'll pray awhile." Smiling, he got up to tend his little ones.

At the Bavith, Ben had lost interest in escape or in time itself. Over and over he ran through the accounts of Haben Jah's life, of all He had said and done. Ben could read quickly, having trained himself early in his career to devour volumes of material, to glean the important facts and details. He had raced through the Basar, that portion of the Kathab that dealt primarily with Haben's earthly ministry. He could see there was a lifetime of study there; a lifetime and beyond. Ben had continued from the Basar to scan the events that had happened after Haben Jah departed; there he discovered Kadosh Neshamah, His purpose and place in the scheme of things. Among the pages he met Sha'uwl, a man breathing out fire against the followers of Haben Jah. Ben found him uncomfortably familiar. His circumstances, too, began to take on an air of familiarity that Ben disliked. Here was a man bent on destroying those who swore allegiance to Haben Jah, who made a full turn and became one of Haben's strongest defenders. He especially found Sha'uwl's end disconcerting, an end marked by imprisonments, beatings, and death. But he couldn't deny the satisfaction the man had evidenced: the total peace he experienced in spite of surroundings. And what had made the difference? Meeting Haben Jah face-to-face on the road to Darmeseq. One encounter and three days' prayer.

Ben shook his head. A life changed; a life that stayed changed. It was what Adamson had said. Haben Jah called it being "born again." New birth to new life. But

was that really possible? Haben Jah said it was. His followers showed it in their lives. How else could cowards
who ran at the time of their Lord's arrest suddenly become fireballs of courage, proclaiming that Haben Jah
lived? Men who couldn't or wouldn't stand for the Truth
when He walked with them, happily faced death for what
many called a lie. Was it possible? Or was it merely a fa-
ble, a fairy tale?

Was Adamson a fairy tale? No. Obviously not. Nor were
the hundreds of other Chasidim who Ben had helped
eliminate. They had died, not in fear, but often praying
for forgiveness for their persecutors. Like Nezer, who
died at Sha'uwl's feet. Like Haben Jah Himself. What
kind of man would do that?

Outside, night had almost come to an end. It was the
hour before dawn. The long darkness was over.

Ben slid the Kathab back into his satchel, resting his
hand lightly on it. There was no need to keep reading; at
least not now. He had the information he wanted; or at
least what he'd needed when all this began. Who was Kadosh Neshamah? Haben Jah. Who was Haben Jah? The
King, come to lay down His life for His people. Who were
His people? Those who accepted Him, who believed in His
name, in His word, and put their faith in Him.

And knowing all that, even believing all that to be true,
Ben knew it still wasn't enough. He could intellectually
walk away from all this . . . well, figuratively speaking, of
course. There was still the matter of the locked room. But
he could leave his studies believing Haben Jah was the
son of the King and remain exactly as he was when he
started. He knew the Truth, and the Truth would not set
him free. Unless . . . . The Truth would set him free only
when he acted on it. If he acted on it. Ben remembered
what the the Kathab said, "You say you believe in the
King? Well and fine. Demons believe, too, and they tremble." Ben had trembled, too. But he didn't have to. He
could change. If he wanted to. Did he?

Ben stared at the satchel for a long time, quietly assessing and reassessing all he'd heard, read, and been through in the past . . . two days. Had it only been two days? It felt like an eternity. What choice would he make? He'd run to Haben Jah out of fear and a desire for self-preservation. Haben Jah hadn't turned him away, but Ben knew He hadn't accepted his pledge of "I'll do anything" as proof of fealty, either.

No, the decision still lay before him.

Ben spoke softly, "I know You're here, and You're listening. I want You to know, if I choose You, it's not because I'm expecting You to rescue me, or anything like that. Not this time." His circumstances truly had no bearing on the decision. People who chose to follow Haben Jah died with regularity. People who didn't lived long, apparently happy lives. But what kind of lifetime would he live, if he knowingly and openly rejected the One Who could give him the peace and freedom he really wanted? What would eternity be like knowing the same thing? "How shall we escape, if we neglect so great a salvation?" How indeed?

Ben nodded to himself. "I know. I know what I have to do." He looked up at the ceiling and said aloud, "I believe You are the son of the King. I want You to be Lord of my life. I'm sorry I doubted You, denied You, refused You . . . everything. I'll make it right if I can. But I believe. Forgive me, Haben Jah."

The words sounded so plain, so unemotional and cold. But Ben felt a wave of emotion sweep through him. His eyes clouded, he closed them tightly. He repeated softly, "I am sorry. Please, please forgive me."

The voice from the alley said strongly, "I already have, My son."

Ben opened his eyes. Through the blur he saw Haben Jah standing before him. Ben fell to his knees, "Lord, Haben Jah."

Haben Jah placed a hand on the man's head and said

calmly. "Peace, son. Be at peace. And be free. Enter into My joy."

Ben bowed his head, unable to speak. He settled back on his haunches as Haben Jah continued, "Today you chose Me. But I chose you long ago to be a special vessel for My own use. I have a place and purpose for you. Dark valleys are yet ahead, but be of good cheer. I am with you always, to the end of the age. I have sent you a Comforter, One Whom you already know. He will guide you into all truth and bring to your remembrance that which I have said. You will never be alone."

Ben nodded and whispered, "I know. Thank You." He looked up and asked, "What do I do? How can I serve You?"

Haben Jah smiled. "You will know. Peace I leave you, My son."

Ben heard the door handle turning. He glanced quickly at the door, then back to Haben. But the Lord was gone; the room empty. No, not empty. Never empty again. Ben turned to face the door.

Mirmah pushed the door open. He snorted at Ben's position on the floor and said roughly. "It's too late for prayer, Ramah. You should have thought of that a long time ago." Mirmah motioned brusquely, "Let's go."

Ben rose slowly, gathering his satchel. His hand slid across the comfort of the Book inside. It gave him a measure of reassurance. He walked quietly forward and stepped outside the room, offering no resistance.

Leah waited in the hall. She looked like she'd had a hard night. Dark circles ringed her eyes; her face was drawn and pale. But the woman stared at him as he came out, meeting his eyes with full defiance. Ben looked back calmly. There was no feeling of malice, anger, or bitterness in him. Only peace. He nodded to her and even smiled slightly, "Hello, Leah."

Leah studied him intently. Ben gazed back calmly. Leah seemed to search his face and eyes, but whatever she was looking for, she didn't find. After a few moments she dropped her eyes and said curtly, "The deal has been made. Adam Chata has agreed to take you in exchange for Arek and the others."

Ben asked quietly, "Is Adamson going to be released as well? Were you able to buy his freedom, too?"

Leah looked up sharply. That wasn't the response she'd expected. She hesitated, then said slowly, "Yes. Conditionally, of course, but he stays alive."

Ben nodded. "I see. Where is the exchange to take place?"

Leah began searching Ben's eyes again. Looking for the man she'd known before, he guessed. Ben wondered where his old self had gone. Would it be back? Leah faltered slightly but admitted, "Town square. After sunrise."

That sounds right, Ben thought, then asked, "Did he say what he intends for me?"

Mirmah laughed harshly. "He's going to promote you, of course." He looked at Leah. "There isn't time for all this chitchat. It's almost dawn. Let's get down to the square. I've got other things to do."

Leah couldn't take her eyes off Ben's face. She searched it one last time, then said very slowly, "I know. Let's go."

She stepped back to allow the men to pass. Ben felt a deep sense of satisfaction at her confusion. It meant she saw something different. Which meant it had really happened. He *was* different. He was a new creation.

Ah, but for how long? Life as he knew it was going to be very short once he was returned to Adam Chata. How long was he going to enjoy this new life?

Ben silenced the taunts inside with a smile. *Forever. I'm going to enjoy it forever.* Eyes sparkling, he walked ahead of his betrayers, down the hall and out the door.

Day of Reckoning

The town square was already full an hour before dawn. Normally workdays in Tebel-Ayr began lazily, but this morning was different. Public gatherings were reserved for special occasions. It was only when word was sent forth that something unique was to occur that the masses came out in droves. And word had gone forth. Adam Chata had a new revelation. Glory of glories, what a privilege to be present when the announcement was made!

The square, designed to hold a thousand people, was jammed with ten times that number. Additional Tabbach guards had been pressed into service to hold back the crowds lest they mob the Governor in their adoration.

People had begun arriving two hours before the call, jostling for the best view. There were no seats. There was no reserved section for prominent personages.

As the last gong vibrated across the now-silent city, Leah, Mirmah, and Ben arrived. Leah had used the secret passages through the catacombs to arrive undetected. No sense testing Adam Chata's dependability prematurely. There would be plenty of opportunity for him to renege later. Which doubtless he would. Leah knew it full well. Then why go through with this?

The woman cut off the argument savagely. She had chosen her course. Leah glared fiercely down the steps. The trio had come out on top of the court of taxes, an unused building which overlooked the square. From here they could see without being seen. Or so it was hoped. Leah tried to determine how Chata would enter the

square. He never arrived from the same direction twice.
That the final call was over, and he wasn't present, was
odd. Especially this morning. Leah frowned. How like the
man; keep everyone guessing.

Leah peered anxiously around the square, ignoring the
silence of the crowds. Where was Arek? She could see
knots of soldiers, and wondered if the Chasidim were being closely guarded in their midst. Chata had agreed she
would be able to see Arek and the others, though they
would not see her, before the announcement of their release. Chata was to vow to release them when Ramah
came forward. His public admission was the assurance
Leah wanted most. Not even Chata could disavow words
spoken five minutes previously in full view and hearing
of half the population of Tebel-Ayr. He'd hold to his word,
as long as Leah held to hers. And she would. It gave her
pleasure to see Ramah cringe and cower. . . .

Except he wasn't. The man was so totally calm, Leah
distrusted it. She sneaked a glance at Ben's face one last
time. There was no fear in his eyes, no anger or apprehen-
sion in his expression. *What had gotten in to him? Had
someone gotten to him? Or Someone?*

Again Leah shook off the thoughts. It didn't matter. Either way, Ben Ramah was out of her life. Permanently.
Good riddance.

Behind her, Mirmah snarled impatiently, "Where is
the Governor? He said he'd be here."

"He'll be here. He wouldn't miss this opportunity for
anything." Leah couldn't disguise the disgust she felt.

Ben suggested helpfully, "He'll come in about twenty-
five minutes late. It makes him look more important."

Leah snorted, "You'd know, wouldn't you?"

Ben nodded. "Yes." He offered nothing more.

Leah stared hard at the man. Ben appeared not to notice but concentrated his gaze on the crowd. Leah gave
him one last long look, then turned to Mirmah. "You can
leave if you like. Ramah isn't going anywhere."

Mirmah shook his head. "I want in on the recognition when he's captured. Turning in such a dangerous criminal will most assuredly be worth a few points on my next evaluation. I'm not leaving yet."

"Suit yourself." Leah turned away from him with disdain. Self-seeking to the last. Like someone else she . . . .

Leah slapped the thought mentally. She'd hear it again, she was sure. Probably in chorus. Leah went back to watching the square.

As Ben had predicted, Adam Chata arrived late. Leah sensed him before she saw him. His presence was dominating, even in a crowd of this size. He walked alone, without guard or escort. But the masses parted automatically as he advanced to the stone platform that marked center square. The platform was only five feet high and three feet round. A series of steps were carved in the stone. The platform might have supported a statue in days gone by. But its original purpose had been forgotten; now it was simply used to deliver new teachings.

Adam Chata walked silently to the center of the square and waited patiently for silence. Leah noted he did not search the crowd for her. Either his spies had already informed him of her presence, or he was totally trusting of her word. Leah wasn't sure she liked either supposition. Maybe she *should* stand him up, make him look the complete fool. No, too late for that. Mirmah would never go for it. Play it out.

A gong sounded. Adam Chata stepped onto the first step. A slight buzz ran through the crowd. Chata smiled benevolently at the masses around him, reached out and shook one man's hand. He laid his palm on a small child's head in paternal blessing, then mounted the second step.

Leah hissed angrily, "Get on with it!"

Ben said, "He's priming the crowd. The master showman at work. It'll be another five minutes before he's ready."

Leah glared at Ben. "Are you enjoying this?"

Ben shook his head. "Not at all. I know the man, that's all. I've seen him work this way for years."

Leah jeered, "And you taught him everything he knows, right?"

"Not hardly." Suddenly Ben smiled, as a thought occurred to him. He nodded slightly and said softly, "No, I didn't. I didn't create Adam Chata. I don't have to take responsibility for that. He was a master long before I ever came on the scene. You can't blame him on me."

Leah sneered, "You're completely innocent, right?"

"No. You just can't blame him on me. There are plenty of other crimes I will answer for. But not him." Ben stared off over the crowd at the figure below. He whispered, "Not him."

Leah acted shocked. "Ben Ramah admitting he's been wrong? What is the world coming to?"

Ben shrugged, maintaining the newfound composure. "Better days, possibly." He smiled and added softly, "For some of us, anyhow."

Leah gave him a sidelong look of distrust. Something was definitely wrong with the man. If this was a ploy to confuse her, it was working. If it was designed to work on her sympathies, it would fail. She had none.

Adam Chata had reached the top of the platform and was standing with his arms outstretched, welcoming and blessing the people. A cheer went up, beginning low from the outskirts of the crowd and climbing higher and higher as more and more voices picked up the refrain: "Cha-ta, Cha-ta, Cha-ta." The governor waved and made as if to silence the crowd. His attempt failed; the noise grew louder. He waited, smiling joyfully, tears in his eyes, as the loyal citizens of Tebel-Ayr expressed their love and support.

Mirmah spat and snarled, "This is disgusting."

Ben said evenly, "Get used to it. Turning me in will make you public heroes. Your presence will be required at all future functions like this."

Mirmah whirled and knocked Ben across the face. "Shut up, you! Shut up."

Leah cried sharply, "Enough! Mirmah, hold your temper. Ramah, keep your mouth shut from now on."

Ben wiped the blood from his mouth, then looked at his hand. He stared at the crimson stain a long time, then turned away. Leah heard him whisper softly, as if to himself, "Haben Jah had His blood spilt, too. Forgive him, Lord."

A knife plunged into Leah's stomach. She gasped as if struck herself. Her father's words—the last words she'd ever heard him speak—were those same words. Dear King, what had she done? What had she done?

The crowd had grown quiet, finally, and waited breathlessly for Chata to speak. The governor began softly, "Brothers and sisters, dearly beloved friends and comrades, greetings. I bring you peace and tidings of great joy. The day we have all longed for, worked for, waited and wept for . . . that day of total harmony and peace is upon us. The kingdom is at hand. It is within you, within me, within each and every one of us. This we have known for decades, indeed, for centuries. But the fulfillment of the reality has been blocked, lo, these many years, by one man, and one man alone."

Leah barely heard the governor's words. She felt physically ill. She wanted to run screaming from the rooftop; maybe to throw herself off the rooftop. Anything to silence the accusations inside. What had she done? What had she become? Her father's betrayer; her own worst nightmare. She stared blankly at the crowd, not seeing anything but the blood on her father's face, mirrored on the face of Ben Ramah. Only she was responsible this time. *Dear King . . . .*

Chata was continuing his speech. ". . . Today, the promise of our release from him who troubles us is at hand." Chata motioned to the crowd, at the same time signaling his guards. Soldiers separated the crowd and marched forward. Ahab, Chedvah, Arek, and Nathan Adamson were brought to the platform, from the four corners of the square. Chata waited until the men stood beneath him, then gazed at them in extreme sorrow. The crowd watched in silent wonder, recognizing the three Chasidim leaders. Chata's voice was full of emotion as he choked, "My sons, my sons. How often would I have gathered your children together, as a hen gathers her brood under her wings. But you would not, and so your houses have been left desolate. Still, I would have mercy on you, my sons. Your lives are to be spared, by the intercession of one more worthy than you all."

Chata glanced up to the roof where Leah stood, picking her out without hesitation. Leah's sickness increased. He'd known where she was all along; known she would come. Birds of a feather. Chata pointed to her; the crowd buzzed and began to look where the governor was pointing.

Mirmah hissed, "That's our cue. Let's go." He shoved Ben towards the steps but noticed Leah wasn't moving. He grabbed her arm roughly and shook her. "Snap out of it, Leah. We're on, so let's go. Move."

Half dragging the woman, Mirmah directed Ben and Leah down the steps, out into the crowd. As they reached the street level, Leah snatched her arm away from Mirmah. She was breathing hard, struggling to resolve the raging conflicts within. She glared hard at Mirmah and hissed, "Don't you touch me! I can do this alone."

Mirmah seethed back, "Sure you can. I saw you freeze on the roof. You aren't backing out now."

"Who said anything about backing out?" Leah turned away from Mirmah and snapped, "Its too late for anything else."

As they walked through the crowd, Ben urged softly, "It's not too late, Leah. Don't do this to yourself." Leah eyed him in confusion and fear. Ben continued, "I'll go forward and the deal's done. I'm not afraid anymore. But save yourself. Turn and walk away."

Leah stopped walking, oblivious to the crowd around her. Not even Mirmah's angry mutters motivated her forward. She stared hard at Ben and saw true concern in his eyes. She choked, "Why? Why do you care?"

Ben shrugged. "I'm not sure. Maybe because someone cared for me, once." He laid his hand on her arm and urged again, "Walk away, Leah. Do it. Walk away. Go home. This isn't you."

Leah turned away to hide the tears that threatened her vision. "You don't know who I am."

"Do you?"

Leah refused to answer. She bit her lip, then choked, "It's too late. Let's go." Resolutely she pushed forward.

Trapped

They arrived at the platform. Adam Chata extended his hand to Leah. She took it and joined him on the pillar. The crowd grew silent again, waiting for an explanation. Guards closed in around Ramah, forming a circle around the man.

Adam Chata addressed the crowd again. "One man has opposed us. He has worn countless faces through the ages, yet always appears to trouble and disrupt our new order. Since I have been governor, he has not ceased to undermine and destroy all I have tried to build; all *we* have tried to build. Yet never was it possible to stop him, until today. Through the diligence and persistence of this one gifted and anointed woman, this man's current incarnation has been revealed to me. Because of this woman's loyalty and devotion to the new order, she has brought our adversary to us, to be finally and irrevocably eradicated."

The crowd began to cheer. Leah's eyes were haunted as she looked into the happy faces of the thousands beneath her all waiting to acclaim her greatness and goodness. She glanced down and saw blood on her hand. Probably Ben's. Angrily she wiped at it, but it didn't come off.

Chata continued his speech. "It has been revealed that the one who stands against me—against us, dear brothers and sisters—is one who has been closest to me. How else could he know so intimately my hopes, dreams, and desires for you, my friends? How else was it possible for him to restrain us at every turn, to block all our efforts at progress and reform? Only one close to me; a man trusted and beloved, raised up as my familiar friend, could hurt me so deeply. A man with whom I have taken sweet counsel together, with whom I have worshiped and prayed. A man, my friend, my son . . . ."

Chata's voice choked with emotion. His pain was evident to see, communicated to every listener and observer. Tears filled his eyes and the governor wept openly. The silence of the crowd grew even deeper, as they watched their governor express his most intimate feelings to them. All present were seeing the very heart of Adam Chata revealed. This was a privileged moment, indeed.

With difficulty the governor regained his composure. He continued finally, "But now it is time to end the struggle. For the higher good of the new order, and the ultimate glory of the king within us, this farce must stop. Now that the plot has been revealed, it can stop."

Chata smiled warmly at Leah, then embraced the woman. Leah was in too much shock and turmoil to resist. None of this was planned, yet none of it unexpected. Chata grasped Leah's hand and held it aloft with his. "Because of this one woman, whom all shall forever call Blessed, we now have the opportunity to end the conflict. Her tireless efforts, her unfailing love and selflessness have provided us with the means to the end we have sought these eons. Her name will be remembered forever as the conqueror of evil, the champion of truth and vision. Leah Bataqab."

The crowd cheered wildly. A name had finally been given to express their joy; they took up the chant: Le-ah, Le-ah, Le-ah. The woman stared at the ground, unable to bear what was happening.

Chata waited a respectful amount of time, then silenced the crowd. He continued, "Our adversary is one man, to be sure, but one man with many hands. For the good of all, it is time to eliminate not only the head, but the hands as well. Because of the pervasive nature of the conspiracy against us, this drastic step must be carried out, grievous though it seems. All who stand in defense of this man must be eradicated. All other crimes may be forgiven, will be forgiven completely. No matter, however great or small, will be judged, except standing in defense of this one man. By this shall men see who is of the order and who is not. It will be the dividing line between the sheep and the goats, the identifier of wheat and tares. All who stand in defense of this traitor must die. All who deny him will live."

Too late, Leah saw the trap Chata was setting. The governor would never openly attack Haben Jah, nor make serving Him the ultimate crime. Not in so many words. But this . . . This would truly divide the faithful. And she'd done it. She had done it, indeed.

Chata addressed the Chasidim leaders, "For your misguided opposition and interference you are hereby forgiven and pardoned. You are free to go wherever you desire. You may continue to teach and preach as is your right in this city. Spread the word of Haben Jah, your master, as you see fit. I give you my blessing." He motioned for the guards to move back, the soldiers melted away into the crowd. Chata smiled at Leah. "I have fulfilled my bargain, dear lady. Your friend is free."

Leah couldn't look at Arek, knowing the pity and compassion she would see there. She didn't deserve it. She'd condemned him. Leah closed her eyes and waited as the trap sprang closed.

Chata motioned for the guards around Ramah to come forward. Ben strode forward without resistance. His gaze was fixed straight ahead, looking into the face of Someone only he could see. Chata stared down at his former assistant and said coldly, "Long have I watched you maneuver and manipulate for your own gain, Ben Ramah. Never until today have I understood why. But now I know. You have taken the essence of Kadosh Neshamah;

you are Neshamah. And henceforth all men shall know it."

Chata raised his voice. "Ben Ramah has betrayed us all. He is the incarnation of Kadosh Neshamah for this age. I have seen it and know it to be true. Anyone who stands in his defense and will deny this truth is a traitor who must die." He motioned again. A soldier came forward, leading Athariym by the arm. Athariym looked around wildly; he had no idea what was about to happen.

Chata addressed him, "Athariym, you have served closely with Ramah. You know him as few others do. Tell me, son, who is Ben Ramah?"

Athariym grasped the straw being offered and yelled, "Neshamah. He is Kadosh Neshamah!"

The crowd buzzed, unsure and uneasy. What were they seeing? More witnesses were brought forward; Ben's former classmates and teachers. All vowed Ben, indeed, was Neshamah. They'd noted the difference in him early on. How else could you describe his rise to power, his genius and ability? Neshamah, to be sure.

The list of witnesses grew longer. Neighbors, acquaintances, former friends, strangers on the street . . . all became anxious to proclaim the truth that Ramah was Neshamah. They'd seen him, heard him, watched him, knew him. The time had come to purge him from their midst. Eagerly they did so.

Mirmah, too, was given his moment in the sun. As the man instrumental in Ben's physical capture, he too was allowed and encouraged to testify to the true identity of Ben Ramah. Mirmah played it for all it was worth.

Only when the crowd was done cleansing itself of Ben's influence did Chata turn to the Chasidim. He winked at Leah and said, "And now, for the final proof." He called aloud, "Nathan Adamson, come forward."

Nathan walked forward. He looked into Ben's eyes and saw the peace there. The two men may as well have been alone, neither saw anyone else. Ben smiled at Nathan, his eyes dancing with relief and joy. Nathan understood the look; he grinned back. Were they not separated by a phalanx of guards, they would have hugged one another. But the recognition was there.

Chata addressed Nathan. "You have sworn service to Haben Jah Himself, and to Kadosh Neshamah, His Spirit. Isn't that how you say it?"

Nathan nodded. His voice was clear and strong as he declared, "I serve the Living God, Haben Jah." Nathan looked back at his newest brother. He saw the pain which clouded Ben's face and knew its meaning. That would be made right, in time. Now that there was time for Ben. All of eternity, in fact.

Adam Chata asked pointedly, "Is Ben Ramah Kadosh Neshamah? You owe this man no allegiance, have no reason to defend him. Is he Neshamah?"

Nathan chuckled. He looked square into Adam Chata's face and said, "He is no more Kadosh Neshamah than I am. We are part of Him, but not the whole."

Chata asked again, more forcefully, "Is Ben Ramah Neshamah?"

Nathan dispensed with all semantic justifications and arguments and said simply, "No, he isn't."

"Then you are defending him."

"Yes, I am."

Chata nodded slowly, then turned to the crowd. "Out of his own mouth, this man has condemned himself. He stands with Ramah and will die with Ramah."

A cheer rose from the crowd. Nathan saw the anguish in Ben's face. He whispered in prayer, "Help him, Lord. Help him understand this wasn't his fault. I know that. Help him know that." Ben's face continued to be stricken, however. Nathan prayed silently, *Wait on Him, Ben, wait on Him. Don't lose hope. Wait on Him.*

Chata motioned towards the Chadisim leaders. The moment Leah had dreaded had arrived; now she would see her friend whom she had schemed to save destroyed by her very plans. The woman dropped her eyes even lower. But no lower than the emptiness inside that engulfed her.

The governor smiled benevolently and addressed Ahab. "You have witnessed the choice before you and the consequences of that choice. What decision will you make?" Chata held up his hand to stop the reply he knew was forthcoming. "Because this should be a day of rejoicing for all my people, I will not demand a response from you. But the day will come when you, and all who hold to the name of Haben Jah, must stand before me and answer. Will you defend a man who for years was your enemy? Or will you deny him, and so save yourselves? Only you can answer that. But not today. Not today, my friends. Go home and think through your reply. Guards!"

Tabbach soldiers escorted the leaders from the square, hustling them out before anyone could utter a word to the contrary. Chata waited until they were gone, then addressed the crowd again. "This is a day of celebration; a day to give gifts to one another, to eat the fat and drink the sweet. Go your ways, my children. Rejoice and make merry. The blessing of the king within be upon you all." Chata stepped down from the platform, bringing Leah down with him. He held her hand tightly as they made their way to the edge of the square. Only when the two had reached the relative seclusion of the square's perimeter did Chata release her. He smiled brightly at Leah and said, "A pleasure doing business with you, my dear princess. I will be in contact with you about our next joint appearance. Have a nice day." Whistling, the governor walked jauntily back to his palace.

Leah stood frozen, unable to move. Crowds passing her by touched her; she didn't notice. She heard some whispering her name; she ignored them. Only when she heard voices call, "There they go. There go the traitors!" did she look up. Ben and Nathan were being led from the square under heavy guard. The crowd threatened to turn ugly, shouting catcalls and jeers as the men were directed away. Someone threw a rock; it hit Nathan in the back of the head. Another rock flew, clipping Ben's shoulder. A cheer went up. Leah closed her eyes, turned and walked blindly away. She could tell each time a stone found its mark—a cheer rose from the crowd. A sob tore from her. Leah began crying and ran.

In the Biryah Prison

Leah sat motionless on the floor of her living room, trying not to think, not to feel, not to be. She wanted to die. Ben Shinown betrayed Haben Jah. In his remorse he had hung himself. Maybe she should, too. But that would only bring her into the presence of the King sooner. The woman shuddered. Lord King, what had she done? In her hatred and desire for revenge, nursed these many years and fulfilled, what had she done? Neshamah had warned her, didn't He? "Continue in your hate, and others will suffer." Well, she'd continued, and now they were. And would continue. Like ripples on a pond.

Leah covered her face with her hands, but no tears came. For whom should she weep? Herself? She got what she wanted. Ben? Nathan? Arek? Who was the real victim?

A loud, angry pounding began at her door. Daniel's knock. Leah remained still. Maybe he'd go away. She couldn't face him. She wouldn't face him.

Daniel pounded again and shouted, "Leah! Open this door. Open it!"

Leah didn't move. He'd go away. Go away. Go.

"Open it, Leah! I know you're here. I'm not leaving. Open the door!"

Leah whispered, "Go away." She closed her eyes and whispered over and over, "Go away. Go. . . ."

She heard the door frame splinter as Daniel slammed against the door, forcing it open. She didn't look up, didn't move as she sensed her brother's presence, menacing and angry. She whispered again, "Go away."

Daniel stared hard at the figure on the floor. The entire range of emotion threatened to overwhelm him, and he couldn't decide what to feel. Anger. Rage. Frustration. Disbelief. Disgust. But also hurt. And pain. And compassion. Love. . . . In the end, what always wins? "Now there are these three: faith, hope, and love. And the greatest of these . . . ."

Daniel knelt down beside his sister. He put his arms around her protectively and said softly, "Oh, Leah."

Leah shook her head. "Go away."

"I can't. Neither can you. Neither will the nightmares. You can't send them away, Leah. Not by yourself."

Leah did not look up, but said hollowly, "No one can."

"Haben Jah can."

Leah looked up into her brother's face. Her eyes were blank, her voice lead, as she said, "I rejected Him. I wouldn't listen. I knew what He wanted, and I rejected Him. He won't help me anymore. It's too late." She dropped her eyes again. "Go away."

Daniel shook his head. "I can't. I love you too much. I won't go away. Neither will Haben. He's here for you, Leah, if you will ask Him."

Leah stared inside herself. Lord King, it was ugly. Ugly and dirty and unclean. She hated it. She hated herself the way she was.

Then why not change? Accept Haben's offer—free offer—of forgiveness and healing and cleansing? She knew the truth. Haben Jah would do all that was promised, if she would only ask. Then why not ask?

Why not? Because she'd have to change, that's why not. She'd have to admit that no matter what had been done to her, no matter how bad it had been, she was the one that was wrong. The others were wrong, too, no question about that. But *she* was wrong. She was a sinner, unclean, unworthy, condemned. To admit her own guilt was to strip her of justification for the way she was. Hate would no longer be right. Nor would jealousy. Wounded pride. Self-ishness. Self-centeredness. Self itself had to be emptied before Haben Jah. She would no more be a free woman, but a servant, a bond slave.

No matter that she was a slave to her own passions now. No matter that in her current "freedom" she had destroyed innocent lives, betrayed all she loved, and sold herself to Adam Chata. Her "freedom" was to choose evil. Was that what she wanted? Freedom to hate, to lie, to cheat, to feed the violent side of her nature which domi-nated her?

Yes! Yes! The thoughts screamed in her head. If being forgiven meant she had to forgive those who had hurt her, she wanted no part of it. Not now, not ever. Never. Never. She'd never forget the wrongs done her. She might say she'd forgive, for it made her the master of the situation. But in her heart of hearts, she treasured the wrongs, locked away until she needed to use them to excuse her actions, or thoughts, or emotions. Surrendering to Haben Jah would mean an end to all that. Because He had suf-fered. He'd been wronged, falsely accused, beaten, spit on, robbed of dignity and, in the end, life itself. He who was truly innocent had borne every sorrow, every pain, every curse. And when His enemies finally hung Him on the tree, what had He done? Forgiven them. It could work for her, too, if she would ask.

Leah looked up at Daniel. Her eyes filled with tears, her voice was small and childlike as she asked, "Will He forgive me? Will He?"

Daniel smiled, a look of relief and hope. He hugged Leah gently and said, "Yes, my sister. Oh, yes. Even now. He forgives you."

Leah buried her head into Daniel's chest and began sobbing. "I'm sorry. I'm sorry. Lord Haben Jah, I'm sorry."

Daniel rocked slightly as a parent to a child, and

soothed her. "It's all right now, Leah. It's all right. It's over. It's over. You're free, Leah. It's over."

Brother and sister sat huddled together for a long time. No one counted the minutes. But eventually Leah looked up at Daniel and said, "I've got to help Adamson and Ramah. I've got to undo what I did, somehow."

"I know." Daniel thought furiously, then suggested, "Let's go to Uncle Nadiyb. As head of the tribe, he can still negate everything you have agreed to." Daniel smiled, without mirth. "It's one of the few traditions from the Kathab Uncle still believes in."

Leah asked, "But will he?"

"I think so. None of what you agreed to directly benefits our people. In light of that, Uncle Nadiyb will probably gainsay it on principle alone. If not, he can annul the agreement and bid for better terms on his own."

"But what do I tell him? How do I explain?"

Daniel studied his sister. His voice was even as he said, "You tell him the truth. That you were wrong, and you want to make it right."

"He won't go for it. Not like that."

"Maybe not, but that's how it's done."

Leah started to say, "Maybe if we . . . ." then stopped. She took a small breath, let it out slowly, and said, "You're right. The truth. I tell him the truth."

"Good." Daniel smiled again. "Haben Jah will help you, Leah. He'll be with you. So will I, for what that's worth. You won't be alone."

Leah didn't try to disguise the relief in her voice. "Good." She sighed slightly. "Let's go, then. There isn't much time left."

"I know. But we do have to wait until at least noon. Uncle Nadiyb isn't home now, remember? This is his morning to hear cases at the Bavith."

Leah groaned. "I forgot. He is presiding judge today. That makes it worse, Daniel. He gets so filled with his own importance, he won't listen to anything."

Daniel reassured his sister. "Leah, Haben Jah knows everything that is happening. Whether Uncle Nadiyb sits as judge today or spends the day in bed it wouldn't make any difference. If we trust Haben Jah, do what we know to do, and leave the rest to Him, He will take care of the outcome. I repeat, we are not alone in this."

Leah nodded reluctantly. "All right, Daniel. We wait until noon. What do we do in the meantime?"

"I have to go to work, at least for the morning. I missed most of yesterday, you know, without explaining where I was. I've got to go back and explain why. And then I'll tell my boss I'll be leaving at noon again today."

"But will he let you go?"

"He'll either let me go today, or he'll let me go, permanently. I think he'll understand."

"What if . . ." Leah stopped herself, shook her head and said, "Haben knows, right?"

"Haben knows."

"What should I do?"

"Pray."

"I am."

"No, I mean really pray. There is a story in the Kathab, when the 'Ibriy wanted to rebuild the temple after its first destruction. The man responsible for trying to start the project worked for the reigning King. He had to get permission, first. The Kathab records his words: 'I prayed to God, then spoke to the King.' "

Leah said in a small voice, "It's been a long time since I've prayed, Daniel. Really prayed, like you said."

Daniel smiled gently. "Then now is the time to start. But remember this, as a wise woman told me last night, prayer isn't making a list of things you want and demanding they come to pass. Prayer is telling Haben Jah what is on your heart, then listening to what is on His."

"I'll remember that."

Daniel grinned. "One of us should. I've got to go. I'll meet you at Uncle Nadiyb's at noon."

"I'll be there."

Daniel gave her a reassuring hug and said, "So will Haben. I'll see you later."

Daniel rose from the floor, then walked quickly out the door. Leah moved from sitting to kneeling, folded her hands and closed her eyes. She hesitated a moment, then said softly. "I'm here, Lord. I'm sorry for the trouble I've created. Show me what to do. Please. Please." Leah sat back to listen.

Nathan and Ben were marched to the lower levels of Biyrah, to the little-used prison section of the palace. The cells were below ground level, without windows of any kind. The walls were solid stone, not pieced together, but of singular construction. No loose bricks to encourage escape attempts or give hope of any kind. Each cell was a roomy four feet by eight feet; enough room to move, not enough to enjoy. A single portal in the door allowed communication with the outside world. A wide corridor ran the length of the prison, with cells on both sides. Two-foot partitions jutted out from beside the doors, effectively isolating each unit. The walls were of ancient construction and absorbed sound. No sense tapping out messages; no one could hear anything. The only respite from the solitude was the prisoner directly opposite you.

By accident, chance, or design, Ben and Nathan were placed in cells across from each other. Perhaps Adam Chata hoped to amuse himself with playing the betrayer against the betrayed. Or perhaps he had no part in the decision, and Someone else directed the placement, for purposes of His own. But Nathan breathed a sigh of relief as he saw what had happened. At least he could talk to Ben. He had to know for sure if what he'd seen in the town square meant what he thought it did. It also gave him the opportunity to encourage his brother, if brother he was.

Nathan waited until the guards were out of sight, then called, "Ben. Ben, come to the door."

There was a long moment's silence. Nathan waited patiently. At last Ben's head appeared in the small window. His eyes still wore the haunted look. Nathan smiled easily. "I told you we'd meet again."

Ben couldn't quite meet Nathan's eyes. He said slowly, "I didn't turn you in, Nathan. I swear I didn't."

"I know that." Nathan shrugged. "I turned myself in."

Ben looked up sharply, "What?"

"I turned myself in."

"Why?"

"Seemed like the thing to do at the time."

Ben smiled sourly, finally. "You would."

Nathan smiled. "Well, . . . I had this idea that I could barter for the others."

Ben grunted slightly, "Now that's a novel thought."

"It worked, didn't it?"

"Worked for who?"

Nathan shrugged again, "Look, I wanted the chance to talk to you again, and I got it. So something went right, somewhere."

Ben couldn't help it. He grinned, "I guess something did."

Nathan studied the younger man, then said, "You met Haben Jah."

The sudden glow in Ben's eyes was all the answer Nathan needed. Ben smiled widely and said, "I met Haben Jah. I serve Him, now. Thanks to you."

Nathan shook his head. "Not me. I had nothing to do with it. The King called you; Neshamah drew you; and Haben Jah received you. He did all the work. I just got to share, that's all."

"But if you hadn't, I might not have known. So thank you, anyhow." Ben's voice grew somber again. "I wish it could have been different. There's too much trouble that will come of this. And it's all because of me."

Nathan said quietly, "Ben, listen to me." Ben dropped his head slightly. Nathan said more strongly, "Listen to me, brother. Haben Jah has always allowed or caused His followers to be tried and tested as if by fire. Sometimes *by* fire. Persecution comes to show who is truly on His side. It's easy to believe when things are going smoothly. But a faith that won't stand troubles isn't faith. Haben Jah wants His followers to know that what He promises is true. These times, bad as they may seem, are still part of His plan. You didn't cause anything Haben can't or won't use for His ultimate purposes and to bring honor to Himself." Nathan paused, letting his words sink in. He continued after a moment. "Did you read the Kathab like I asked? "

Ben looked up again, trying to figure where Nathan was leading. "Yes, most of it. I couldn't get in depth with it, though."

Nathan smiled. "That's a job for a lifetime, not a one-time reading."

"I figured that out."

"Good." Nathan grinned. "You're ahead of some of the Chasidim I know." He grew more serious. "Maybe you remember the very first description of Haben Jah, of what it was He came to do. It was announced by Haben's prophet. He said Haben would come as with fire, that '. . . His fan is in His hand, and He will thoroughly purge His floor, and gather His wheat, but the chaff He will burn with unquenchable fire.' Haben Himself said He'd come to set brother against brother, family against family. Serving the King isn't easy; it's warfare. This life isn't a playground, it's a battlefield."

Nathan stopped. He grinned self-consciously and added, "End of lecture. But you get the idea. Persecution didn't start with you; it won't end with you either. It's part of His plan, for now."

A voice from the corridor startled both men. "Ah, yes,

part of the plan. I thank you so very much for participating in it. You played your parts admirably."

Adam Chata stepped forward, smiling triumphantly. He nodded to each man in turn, then focused on Nathan. "Your refusal to identify Ramah as Neshamah has set a wonderful precedent. Your death will punctuate the statement for all to see." Chata's eyes narrowed slightly. "As for your son; well . . . I wager he returns to this city and to my service within the week. And you can enjoy eternity knowing you allowed him to perish."

Nathan quoted quietly, " 'None that you have given Me have I lost.' Haben Jah knows how to save my son. He's the only one who can; the only one who ever could. Kill me. I won't serve you."

Chata nodded. "I intend to. Tomorrow, about this time. A public execution of a traitor so vile the world will be glad of your removal." Chata smiled. "Oh, the evils you will have committed in your past!"

Nathan snorted. "I'm sure you'll be quite creative in your slanders. It doesn't matter. I stand before the King. He knows."

Chata chuckled. "Of course, of course. Comfort yourself with that, friend. It's all the pleasure you will get." Chata turned to Ben. He studied his former aide a long time, then said, "Ben, Ben. I had such hopes for you. You were to be my replacement after I was gone. Governor Ben Ramah. Wasn't that always your ultimate goal, to take my place?

Ben looked at the Governor. The long-avoided and much-feared confrontation was about to take place, and there was only peace inside. Peace. Tranquility, a sense of confidence and sureness he'd never known before. He raised his head a little higher, stood a little straighter, and said, "Yes, it was. Once. Not anymore. I serve the true King now."

Chata laughed heartily, "Oh, yes, I know. I do know." His voice hardened slightly. "The only king you have ever served was yourself. You serve him still. You think throwing yourself on Haben Jah in time of dire trouble will win His favor? You see Haben as another escape, another out from your circumstances. Except it won't work. I hold the key, Ramah. I hold the keys to the kingdom of power you desire. You can still have them, you know."

Chata drew closer to Ben's cell, up to the window itself. He lowered his voice so Nathan couldn't hear, and urged, "You can still save yourself, Ramah. Adamson is lost; you don't have to be. All can be forgiven. I can yet change what was and redeem you from death. I have that power. Renounce this foolish plan of yours and come back. Why destroy yourself? And what about others? You can save them by saving yourself. It's all there for you, if you'll take it. Think about it. Think hard about it, my son. I offer you life. I *am* life for you. Come to me."

Ben stared hard at Chata. Niggling doubts began to reach him. Was he so sure about Haben? Was he really?

Chata stepped back, folded his hands behind his back and said, "Well, I must be off. I will see you gentlemen tomorrow at dawn. It will be another momentous occasion for Golah." Chata breathed a deep sigh of contentment. "Ah, the glory of it all!" Smiling, the man walked out of sight.

Nathan waited impatiently for Chata to be gone, then started to call for Ben. But a quiet voice behind him said, "Let him be. It is not you that must encourage him now."

Nathan turned to face Kadosh Neshamah. "Then what do I do?"

"Pray for him."

Nathan turned back to stare at the cell across the way. "I will. I will."

Freedom

All of Tebel-Ayr was buzzing with confusion, excitement, fear, and expectation. Town criers carried the word swiftly to the edges of the city and back again. The gauntlet had been thrown down, the line drawn in the sand for all to declare their allegiance. Work was stopped. Adam Chata had declared it a holiday, but even the pleasure houses were empty as people milled in the streets, trying to make sense of the new revelation.

For the commoner, it meant little. If Adam Chata declared Ben Ramah was Kadosh Neshamah, so what? If the Governor declared the sky was purple with pink spots, it mattered little. Until it directly impacted the individual, what mattered? As long as there were jobs to fill, what the Governor declared about anyone or anything was inconsequential.

For those who knew Ben Ramah, it was another story. Decisions must be made, futures determined. What did they owe Ben? Friendship? Loyalty? What would they lose by supporting him? Their lives. By denying him? Well, . . . nothing, really. They would be better off, in fact. Those dark secrets Ben knew, for example. They would go to the grave with him. And since Adam Chata had declared Ben a traitor, nothing Ben could say would be believed. Who would be foolish enough to try to defend him by securing the proofs Ben had, anyway? No, better all around to see him go.

The Chasidim, too, had decisions to make. The separate houses called emergency meetings to discuss the events in the square. In some houses there was no debate. It wasn't a question of would they deny Ramah was Neshamah, but when would they come forward? Should they go now, today, or wait until the issue was pressed? Prayers were offered for guidance and for strength to do what must be done. In those houses, members left with a sense of peace, of calm assurance that all things work together for good, for them that are the called according to His purpose.

Other houses, though, experienced more turmoil. Adam Chata had been correct in saying the issue of Ben Ramah would separate the wheat from the tares, weeds that merely looked like wheat. More than a few members of the Chasidim were reluctant to defend Ben Ramah. After all he had done to them? Not for anything in this world would they die on his behalf. As to the next world, well . . . the King would forgive them. He promised to forgive them, didn't He?"

Ah, but He also promised to discipline those who were truly His. So cautioned wise heads in the faith. You can't claim Haben Jah as Lord, then live as the unbelievers do. Not and get away with it forever. You cannot accept Haben Jah in word, but deny Him in action. Do not be deceived; God is not mocked. What you sow, you reap.

Appeals to faith and wisdom pricked the hearts of some, fell on deaf ears in others. Like a tree shaken in a mighty wind, leaves and branches that were rooted and grounded remained, while the dead weight blew away. So it was. "Abide in Me," Haben said. Some houses grew closer and stronger because of the challenge. Others disappeared completely. None remained untouched, as the Lord intended. All things do work together for good.

Leah swallowed hard as she faced her uncle. Nadiyb was seated at his dinner table, having finished his lunch moments earlier. As with a king in his court, Leah and

Daniel waited respectfully for him to motion to them, signaling they could petition him. Leah thought she read satisfaction in her uncle's eyes, but that could have been her own interpretation. She had often misread Nadiyb. Now, however, wasn't the time. She prayed silently, *This time, please. This time, I want to do it Your way. Help me.*

Nadiyb waved Leah and Daniel forward. Daniel squeezed Leah's hand tightly as they came up to the table. She smiled nervously at her brother, then took a deep breath. Now for it.

Nadiyb asked, "Do I guess why you are here? Or do I assume it has something to do with the spectacle at the square this morning?"

Leah swallowed hard. The lump wouldn't go down. Oh, well. Onward and upward. "It does."

"That was quite a show you put on out there. You must be very proud of yourself." Disgust was heavy in Nadiyb's voice.

Leah straightened slightly. "I'm not. I was wrong. I should never have been there. I shouldn't have turned Ramah in."

Nadiyb stared at Leah, aghast. "Be still, my heart! Can this truly be my niece, Leah, admitting error? No, not possible. Not my niece. She's never wrong."

Leah bit her tongue, then repeated, "I was wrong. I've been wrong about a lot of things. I want to make it right. I need your help."

Nadiyb grabbed at his chest. "What? What? Not only admitting error, but asking for help? Oh, this is too much for an old man. Can I stand the strain?"

Daniel said sharply, "Uncle!"

Leah stopped her brother. "No, Daniel, he has a right to mock me. I've mocked him many times. Let him enjoy his triumph." Leah stared calmly at her uncle. "Take what pleasure you will, Uncle Nadiyb."

Nadiyb studied his niece, then grew serious. Maybe he saw his sarcasm was having no effect, so he dropped it.

His voice took on a tone of disinterest as he asked, "Why this change of heart? You maneuvered Ramah splendidly. You made a name for yourself and can choose your own path from here. What went wrong?"

"All of it was wrong. Ramah isn't Neshamah, any more than you are. I wanted to try to save Arek and the others. I didn't realize Adam Chata would twist it to destroy them."

Nadiyb shrugged. "You live and you learn. Play with fire . . . ."

Leah finished it. ". . . and you get burned. But it wasn't me that got hurt. I want to change it, Uncle Nadiyb. I want to make it right."

"What do you expect *me* to do?" There was open disdain in Nadiyb's voice.

Leah pushed ahead. "You can talk to Adam Chata. You hold sway with the 'Ibriy and he knows it. Tell the governor I was wrong, and that his plan won't work. Tell him he will lose favor with your people if he persists in his plans. That the 'Ibriy won't stand by and allow the Chasidim to be destroyed for no reason. You can do it, Uncle. He'll listen to you."

The urgency in Leah's voice was apparent to all present. She pleaded openly, "I'm asking you, Uncle. Please. Stop the madness."

Nadiyb eyed his niece with growing interest. His eyes narrowed. "And what will you give in exchange for this act of mercy on my part? You know I have no love for the Chasidim. Why should I stand up for them? Adam Chata is about to remove them from existence. Why should I stop him?"

Leah squared her shoulders. "Because it's wrong, that's why. The 'Ibriy have had differences with the Chasidim. But the Chasidim have stood by your people when no one else would. And that's history. What matters now is now. If the Chasidim are destroyed, how long before Chata turns to remove the 'Ibriy?"

Nadiyb waved it off. "Inconsequential. No kingdom has ever been able to stand against the 'Ibriy. We will remain, Leah. A remnant will always remain."

Daniel said quietly, "A faithful remnant. Those who serve the King in truth. You aren't among them, Uncle. You know it, and so do we."

The challenge was so quiet Nadiyb missed it at first. When he caught it, he sat up hard. His voice thundered, "How dare you insult me in my home?"

Daniel continued to keep his voice low and calm. "Because it's true. And here is more truth. If the Chasidim are to be destroyed, I will be in the forefront of those who die. I serve Haben Jah, Uncle. I have since father took us to Amanah. I made my decision, then, and I've never renounced it." Daniel looked Nadiyb straight in the eyes and said, "You killed your brother for making that choice. Will you now kill his son for the same decision?"

Leah stared at Daniel in fascination. Her voice was awestruck as she whispered, "You knew? You knew?"

Daniel nodded. "I knew." He stared levelly at Nadiyb. "I've known for two years how you engineered the cave-in that was to take Father's life. Except he wasn't ever alone that night. Your plan didn't go right, did it? Not when the other men were caught, too. They were able to dig free. Dad was hurt. When Mom came, the two of them were picked up by you and driven off." Daniel's voice became even softer as he said, "No one saw them after that. You murdered them, didn't you? Murdered your brother and his wife."

Nadiyb studied Daniel. "How did you come to this knowledge?"

"It doesn't matter. I hated you when I found out. I wanted to kill you. Haben Jah had to show me that murdering you in my heart was no different than what you had done in reality. I was no better than you. I had to forgive you and get on. I did."

Leah's eyes brimmed with tears. She whispered, "You didn't tell me."

Daniel smiled sadly at his sister. "I couldn't. Not then. You were consumed with enough hate then; you didn't need that."

Leah closed her eyes and bit her lip. He was right. What would she have done had she known? Leah shuddered.

Daniel addressed his uncle. "Will you now destroy me, too?"

Leah looked up. "And me. I accepted Haben Jah as well."

Nadiyb stared at both of them, his mind turning. After five minutes of intense silence he said thickly, "Leave this house. Never come back here again. I will speak to Chata, but you two are banished from my presence forever. I never want to see you again."

Daniel squeezed Leah's hand. He said, "We'll go. Your secret is safe, Uncle. I would not use it against you, not even to win my life. But there is One Who knows. And you will stand before Him. One day, you will answer for it."

Daniel and Leah turned and walked quickly from the room. As they reached the street Leah stopped and hugged her brother, sobbing softly. "Daniel, I'm sorry. Thank you. Thank you."

Daniel hugged her back, his voice tender. "I love you, Leah."

Neshamah's voice said strongly, "Well done, My children. Well done."

Leah looked into the face of the King, and smiled through her tears. "Thank You, too. I'm sorry I made such a disaster. What more can I do?"

Neshamah said, "You must leave Tebel-Ayr for now. I need you in Yada. There is one who will be journeying to Amanah and will need a strong guide. Go to the river Irijah and wait. Tomorrow at sundown he will be there. Take him across and teach him the road."

Leah had a feeling and asked, "Who is it?"

Neshamah smiled. "Does it matter?"

Leah grinned. "No. I'll be there."

Daniel asked, "And me?"

"Return home. I will call on you." Neshamah disappeared.

Leah hugged Daniel tearfully. "I'd better get going. Give my love to Ruth. Leah asked, "How did it go with your job? Do you still have one?"

"Yes. It turns out that my boss is a friend of Chedvah's. He left work yesterday, too. And since today was officially declared a holiday, it didn't matter that I left. I'll be fine."

Leah nodded. "Good. I'll see you when I get back."

Daniel smiled. "I know you will. Take good care of him."

"I will. You bet I will." Leah smiled and hurried down the street.

Nathan's trial was scheduled for sundown. Two hours before the appointed time, Nadiyb Bataqab sent word he would hold audience with Adam Chata. News stirred the already excited city. The two strongest leaders in all of Golah meeting at last. What more wonderful events could take place on this momentous day? The Governor ordered his guard into full-dress regalia to honor the occasion. The hall of audiences was hastily polished, the royal tapestries were laid along the path, and the palace gates were thrown open wide.

At the agreed upon time, one hour before sunset, Nadiyb arrived at the palace. His entourage included his senior assistants and their scribes, ready to record the historic event. Adam Chata met him at the gate with full honors: ruffles and flourishes on the trumpets, and a sharp drum-roll for added effect. Nadiyb tolerated the embrace from Chata, returning it for posterity's sake. As the two men entered the palace, Nadiyb said in an aside, "This won't take long, Governor. I want to dispense with the formalities once we are inside. Out of eyesight of our common admirers, of course."

Chata nodded. "I understand." He addressed Nadiyb loudly, but for the benefit of the crowd of followers. "Because of the nature of this visit, I wish our communications to be on a personal level. We are equals, you and I, Nadiyb Bataqab. We share the same goals: the good of our people. Why don't we go to my office where we can be free to talk?"

Nadiyb nodded, also speaking for the crowd's benefit. "An excellent idea, Governor." He added, "What purpose would be served in extended demonstrations of friendship and respect? We both know who and what we are." He smiled pleasantly, but his eyes glinted.

Chata said smoothly, "Of course, honored friend. You already know the level of respect and admiration I hold for you and your people." His eyes, too, told a story.

Nadiyb chuckled slightly. "And I, for yours."

Points made, the two men walked silently down the corridor to the Governor's office. They went inside and closed the door, leaving the others to guess what might be taking place.

Chata chose not to sit behind his desk. He sat in the window seat, relaxing as with an old friend. Nadiyb, too, took the casual approach. He turned his chair away from the desk, sat down, then leaned back, letting the chair rest on two legs against the desk. He studied the Governor a moment, then said, "I will come straight to the point. I wish to discuss my niece."

Chata smiled. "Ah, yes. Leah Bataqab. A wonderful young woman."

"A foolish imbecile." Nadiyb's voice remained disinterested. "She has stepped far across the bounds of good sense. I have been forced to send her away for awhile, until she regains some measure of her reason."

Chata shrugged. "A pity. I had hoped she and I could work together again."

"So I understand. She is, however, totally unreliable. Fickle. Flighty. She is not a responsible representative for the 'Ibriy."

Chata considered this, then asked, "Would you be willing to recommend someone else?"

Nadiyb shrugged. "If it served a purpose, I suppose I might think of someone."

"What purpose would that be, might I ask?"

Nadiyb's eyes glinted again. "Why, the mutual good of our peoples, of course."

"Of course." Chata's eyes flashed. "And how is the good of your people best served at this time."

"This farce with Ramah." Nadiyb's voice grew bored. "It has upset a good many of my less-enlightened brothers. They are concerned that if you perpetrate this lie to the destruction of the Chasidim, you might eventually try something equally absurd against us. I have sought to reassure them that such would never be the case. You are far too intelligent a ruler to believe you can stand against the 'Ibriy. It has been one of your most redeeming qualities, my dear Governor. But you know how tiresome the little people can be. They insist I speak to you."

Chata absorbed this silently. It was not totally unexpected, though he had thought the protest would come from some other source. He said, finally, "And what is it your little people would have me to do? I cannot unbrand Ramah or Adamson as traitors. To admit error would destroy faith in my wisdom and leadership. That would hardly serve the best interests of my people, now, would it?"

"Oh, of course not. My people are not concerned with Ramah or Adamson. Do with them as you will. Their lives matter not at all. But perhaps both our peoples would benefit if you chose not to pursue this any further. No need to recant or renege, just don't do anything." Nadiyb smiled. "After all, the threat alone is sufficient to accomplish many of your desired ends. Allowing Adamson to die will prove the sincerity of your edict. Simply let it hang there."

Chata considered this. "And how are my people benefited?"

"You win the undying loyalty of your people, the respect of my people, and the perpetual fear of the Chasidim. What more could you want?"

Chata said dryly, "And how do you benefit?"

"I do not." Nadiyb shrugged. "I fulfill a pledge to speak to you. That is all."

"And demonstrate to your people that you can sway the mind of the Governor of Golah? Making yourself more powerful than I am? I think not."

Nadiyb hastened to correct the misunderstanding. "Of course not, Governor. This visit need have nothing to do with today's events. It is a meeting long overdue between our peoples. I would not have anyone know I had spoken on behalf of the Chasidim. Many of my people might read the wrong message in that assumption." Nadiyb let Chata get the full drift of his meaning, then continued, "No, we're just two old men, getting together to discuss matters of mutual interest."

"I see." Chata thought it over, then nodded. "Very well, old man. I will take your advice into consideration. I appreciate your visit today. Perhaps both our peoples will have been well served by it."

Nadiyb stood up. "Let us hope so." He motioned towards the door. "We must solidify our mutual respect for the common good. A joint statement, perhaps?"

Chata stood up as well. "Certainly. But a brief one. I do have a trial to attend."

"Of course, Governor."

Together they walked out into the corridor, arm-in-arm to the delight of the waiting crowd.

The hours passed quickly in the prison at Biyrah. Nathan spent time praying, sleeping, sometimes singing hymns of praise. Ben spent his hours listening, thinking, and sometimes even praying. The last he was unsure of, but he tried. And it seemed to work. When he prayed, the shadows receded. When he thought, they attacked him from all sides. He much preferred the former and worked hard at it. Many times he wanted to call to Nathan for help or support, but didn't. Either Ben believed Haben Jah because He was real, or He wasn't. Being convinced by or for someone else wouldn't help. He had to know that he knew that he knew. The King had no stepchildren, no "I'm with him" followers. Ben believed, or he didn't.

Ben's soul-searching was interrupted when the guards arrived to take Nathan for his trial. The prison door groaned open, and the rhythm of marching feet sounded in the corridor. Ben scrambled up and looked quickly, fearing the death squad had come early. But the soldiers wore the shimmering white of the Governor's guard, not the stark black of the executioner. They stopped at Nathan's door, opened it, and ordered him out. Nathan stepped out without protest, limping badly, but his head high. Ben turned away before Nathan could catch his eye, sank to the floor of his cell, and buried his head in his hands.

The guards marched Nathan down the long corridors, back to the judgment hall. The squad pushed open the door. Nathan stumbled slightly; a soldier caught him and thrust him back up roughly. He hissed, "Up, traitor. Governor Chata wants you to make a good impression tonight."

As the door swung fully open Nathan understood the guard's meaning. The judgment hall was fully lit and packed with spectators. Something different was about to happen tonight, it would seem. Nathan peered around the giant hall, looking for faces he might know. He saw none. The crowd was obviously handpicked. Not uncommon; Adam Chata left nothing to chance if he could help it.

The squad moved forward, marching Nathan to the high seat. Adam Chata was already present, having set the stage earlier with a small address to the crowd. The Governor stared down silently as the squad stopped, unshackled Nathan, then slipped back out of the center of attention. Adam Chata gazed down in pity at Nathan.

Five minutes passed as the Governor and prisoner assessed each other. Finally Adam Chata broke the silence. He ordered, "Recorder, read the charges."

The court recorder stepped back from beside the high seat and read in sonorous tones, "Nathan Adamson, you stand accused of high treason. You have refused to serve the Governor as he has requested. You stand accused of forcibly kidnapping then abandoning two young people, Jonathan and Rachel Adamson." You were instrumental in the betrayal and death of your own wife, Yaldah Adamson. You have advocated and taught rebellion to the new order and have refused to swear allegiance to the Governor of Golah. You have publicly defended one whom the laws of our land condemned, Ben Ramah, taking his part in defiance to the edict against him. You have manipulated and destroyed men of reputation to serve your own ends in your pursuit of public office. You have . . . ."

The recorder droned on. Nathan smiled. The charges were a blend of his former life and his present. The case against him was built on the worst of his old nature, before Haben Jah, and the best of the new, after having become a follower of the Lord. There were no surprises in the charges. The recorder droned on for a full twenty minutes.

Nathan waited patiently for him to finish, praying silently all the while, *Lord, give me the opportunity to declare Your name. If it was for this I returned to Tebel-Ayr, let me not fail to witness for You. Prepare the heart of even one listener, that he might hear and heed Your message of life.* Nathan did not try to rehearse a speech but asked himself, "What would Haben Jah say if He were here right now, on trial in my place?" Of course, Haben Jah wouldn't have to answer "Guilty" to each charge. But what would He say?

The recorder finished, then stepped back. Adam Chata stared hard at Nathan and asked, "How do you answer these charges?"

Nathan said strongly, "For the crimes of my past, committed to serve only my own selfish ends, I plead guilty as charged. For the crimes of the present, committed to serve my Lord Haben Jah, I plead guilty as charged."

A slight buzz ran through the crowd. Adam Chata stilled it with a wave of his hand. He said, "It is not your service to Haben Jah that has condemned you, Adamson. I will not allow you to cloud the issue, hoping to become a martyr for conscience's sake. Your unfortunate allegiance to the old myth is between you and your soul. Haben Jah is not on trial here. You are. You are accused of treason for supporting and defending Ben Ramah. How do you plead?"

"Guilty." Nathan said it loud, clear and strong for all to hear.

Adam Chata nodded in satisfaction. "Then by your own lips you stand condemned. The penalty determined against you is death."

Nathan interrupted boldly. "I was under a death penalty before I met Haben Jah. He removed it from me."

Chata's voice became hard. "This trial is no joke, Adamson. I have the power and right to execute you, as I have the power and right to give you life."

Nathan quoted from the Kathab, " 'Do not fear him who can only kill the body, but fear Him Who can cast both body and soul into Shachath Ya'ash, the pit of hell." You have no power but what is given to you from my King, whose I am and whom I serve. It is Haben Jah that gives life, Governor. And that life no one can take away from me."

Chata's eyes glinted. "The penalty is death. You will be executed at dawn. Then we will see who has life."

Nathan quoted again, " 'To be absent from the body is to be present with the Lord.' To die for my Lord will be a great gain."

Chata sneered, "Then by all means let me help you into His presence. Guards." Chata motioned for the soldiers to come forward and get Nathan.

Nathan smiled. He quoted, " 'What can separate us from the love of Haben Jah? Can death . . . .' "

Chata roared, "Silence him!"

A soldier struck Nathan hard across the face. Nathan crumpled to the floor, tasting blood again. His eyes blurred, and there was no strength in him to stand. Rough hands forced him to his feet, then fairly carried him out through the crowd. Nathan closed his eyes and whispered, "Forgive them, Father. They don't know what they are doing."

A soldier's staff crashed against the back of Nathan's head, and he knew no more. The guards dragged the limp form back to the prison, thrust him into his cell, and let him drop on the floor. As the squad withdrew, one soldier remained behind. He knelt beside the broken figure and tried to straighten him out carefully. The soldier stared intently at the beaten face, then whispered in confused wonder, "Forgive us? Forgive me?"

The squad leader barked harshly, "Assemble!"

The soldier stood to his feet, took one last look at Nathan, then left the cell, still confused. What manner of man was this? What did he mean, Haben Jah had released him from the penalty of death? What manner of Lord did Nathan Adamson serve? Maybe he should find out. If it was important enough to die for, he definitely should find out.

Dawn brought Ben Ramah's deliberations to an end. Eight Tabbach guards tramped down the corridor in tight formation. The death squad. They wore black hoods, black robes, and black boots. Ben knew them well; he'd handpicked most of them. He swallowed hard as they came to the cell door and stopped. As one man they turned and faced Nathan's door. The center guard opened the door and motioned.

Nathan stepped out slowly, in great pain. Ben studied the man intently. There was no fear in his face, only a look of total peace. He smiled at Ben, and said quietly, "I'll meet you again, brother. Look for me at Haben's feet."

Ben caught the eye of Ga'al, the chief executioner. He expected no sympathy and asked none, but requested quietly, "One minute."

Ga'al broke formation, shrugged, and let Nathan approach Ben's door. Ga'al unlocked it; Ben stepped into the corridor. He hugged Nathan tightly, then choked, "I'll be there. I will be there."

Nathan grinned widely. "I knew you would." Nathan straightened as best he could, set his shoulders, and said, " 'I have fought the good fight, I have kept the faith. Henceforth there is laid up for me a crown of righteousness which the Lord, the righteous judge, shall give me.' " He smiled. The guards closed ranks around him. Ga'al shoved Ben back into his cell and pulled the door shut. Ben sank down, unable and unwilling to watch as Nathan walked away. The man was singing, however. Ben could hear him reciting, " 'The Lord is my Shepherd, I shall not want. . . .' "

Ben closed his eyes but couldn't close his mind. He'd seen the executions too often. Nathan would be marched to the center square, given one last opportunity to repent of his crimes against the government and its loyal citizens, then swiftly beheaded. End of story.

Except it wasn't. Not for Nathan. Death was the beginning of eternity with Haben Jah. Eternity in glory. Eternity in peace and joy and light and life. Ben nodded to

himself. It was. No more doubts, no more questions. The
conflict was over, and Haben Jah was Lord.

A vision of Adam Chata filtered into Ben's cell. Ben
stared at the apparition calmly and said quietly, "You
have nothing to offer. Go."

The shimmering spirit urged, "I have life."

"You have death. I will never renounce Haben Jah.
You lose. Now, and forever. Haben Jah is Lord. Be gone."

Neshamah said strongly, "Well done, Ben'el. Well
done."

The vision of Chata vanished instantly. Ben rose to his
feet and stood before Kadosh Neshamah. He faced the
Man and said, "I serve the Risen Lord. I hope my death
will serve You, somehow."

Neshamah smiled gently. "It would. But your life honors Me more at present. Go to the river Irijah. I have appointed a guide to take you across into Yada, the King's
country. There you will be instructed in the ways of the
Lord."

The prison doors swung open silently. Ben stared in
wonder at it, unsure if what he was seeing was real. Neshamah repeated, "Go to the Irijah. No one will hinder
you. I have spoken. Go, My son, and be of good courage.
We will meet again."

Ben stared at the door again. He looked at Neshamah
and asked, "Couldn't You free Nathan as well?"

"Nathan is free, My son. Free forever. He is with the
Lord. Yours is the harder task. Now go."

Neshamah vanished. Ben stepped outside the cell,
walked down the corridor, and out the prison door. No
one was around. Ben's confidence began to grow. He
marched boldly through the streets, joy flooding every
corner of his being. He had been prepared to die for Haben Jah; now he must live for Him. He was accepted. He
was loved. Joy unspeakable and full of glory! There was a
guide waiting, he was going to Yada, then on to Amanah,
and into full service for His King. He whistled softly the

tune Nathan had sung going down the corridor and finished the verse, " '. . . and I will dwell in the house of the
Lord forever.' " Forever! Ben grinned, and fairly ran to
begin his new life in the Lord. He was free at last. The
Truth had set him free. Free, indeed!

The last light of day touched the hills above the Irijah.
Leah was trying to wait patiently, but found herself pacing around her makeshift camp. She was beginning to get
hungry. She heard the sound of footsteps on the trail
above. As the sounds grew closer, Leah turned to watch
the break in the rocks where the trail came around to her
camp. Ben Ramah appeared, looking worn but eager.
When he saw Leah, he stopped, uncertain. Leah ex-
claimed, "*You!*" Then she smiled.

Glossary of Names

'Ab Ramah	father of deception
Adam Chata	man of sin
Ahab	love
Amanah	covenant
Amats	courage
Arek	long-suffering
Athariym	spy
Bagad	unfaithful
Basar	gospel
Batsa	greedy
Bavith	temple
Ben-'el	son of God
Ben Ramah	son of deception
Ben Shinown	son of Simon (Judas)
Biyrah	palace
Chalaq	partner
Chasidim	saints
Chavvah	Eve
Chayah	life
Chedvah	joy
Chen	grace
Dabar	promise
Daniel	judge of God
Darmeseq	Damascus
Dodovah	aunt
Golah	captivity

Haben Jah	The Son of God
Hannah	favored
Heylel	Lucifer
'Ibriy	Hebrew
Irijah	fear of the Lord
Kadosh Neshamah	Holy, Divine Inspiration
Kathab	Scriptures
Kechash 'owb	lying spirit
Kiymah	star
Leah Bataqab	weary, daughter of Jacob
Miriam	rebelliously
Mirmah	treacherous
Nadiyb	liberal
Nahal	guide
Nasi	prince
Nezer	crown (Stephen)
Qadiysh	tomb
Ruth	friend
Samuel	heard of God
Shachath Ya'ash	pit of despair
Shalom	peace
Sharath Shinan	ministering spirit
Sha'uwl	Saul
Shephat	judgment
Tabbach	butcher
Taqan	straight
Tebel-Ayr	city of confusion (Babylon)
Yada	knowledge
Yaldah	girl

All names and terms are from: *Strong's Exhaustive Concordance of the Bible*